Souls of the Dark Sea

Book Two

Saga of the Outer Islands

A. F. Stewart

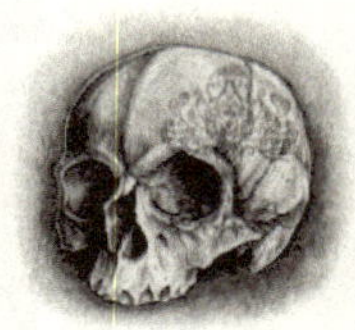

More Books by A. F. Stewart

Multi-Author Anthologies:

Abandon: 13 Tales of Impulse, Betrayal, Surrender, and Withdrawal
A Twist of Fate: A Collection of 11 Twisted Fairy Tales
Beyond the Wail
Legends and Lore
Mechanized Masterpieces
Christmas Lites Series (Books III-VII)
Coffin Hop: Death by Drive-In

Fiction:

Ghosts of the Sea Moon (Saga of the Outer Islands Book I)
Renegades of the Lost Sea (Saga of the Outer Islands Book III)
Chronicles of the Undead
Killers and Demons II: They Return
Killers and Demons
Fairy Tale Fusion
Gothic Cavalcade
Ruined City
Once Upon a Dark and Eerie...
Passing Fancies

Poetry:

Primal Elements: An OWS Ink Poetry Anthology
Horror Haiku Pas de Deux

Horror Haiku and Other Poems
Colours of Poetry
Reflections of Poetry
Shadows of Poetry
Tears of Poetry

Dedication

For those that love the sea and the monsters that lurk in its shadows.

And for Ray Harryhausen whose skeletons inspired me.

Echo Bay
Llansfoot
Pentown
Abersythe
Evermarsh
Temple of Star Reef
Razor Reef
Black Shoals Harbour
Black Shoals
Outcast Key
Silver Haven
Crickwell Town
Red Bay
Crickwell Island
Storm Point
White Fin Point
Sunlight Bay
Cockcrow Bay
Tenby Key
Rock Island
Rock Island Temple
Bay of the Moon
Shadow Cay
Riverford
Blue Bay
Raven Rock
Stone Fire Islands
Deep Sea Key
Red Reef
Old Town

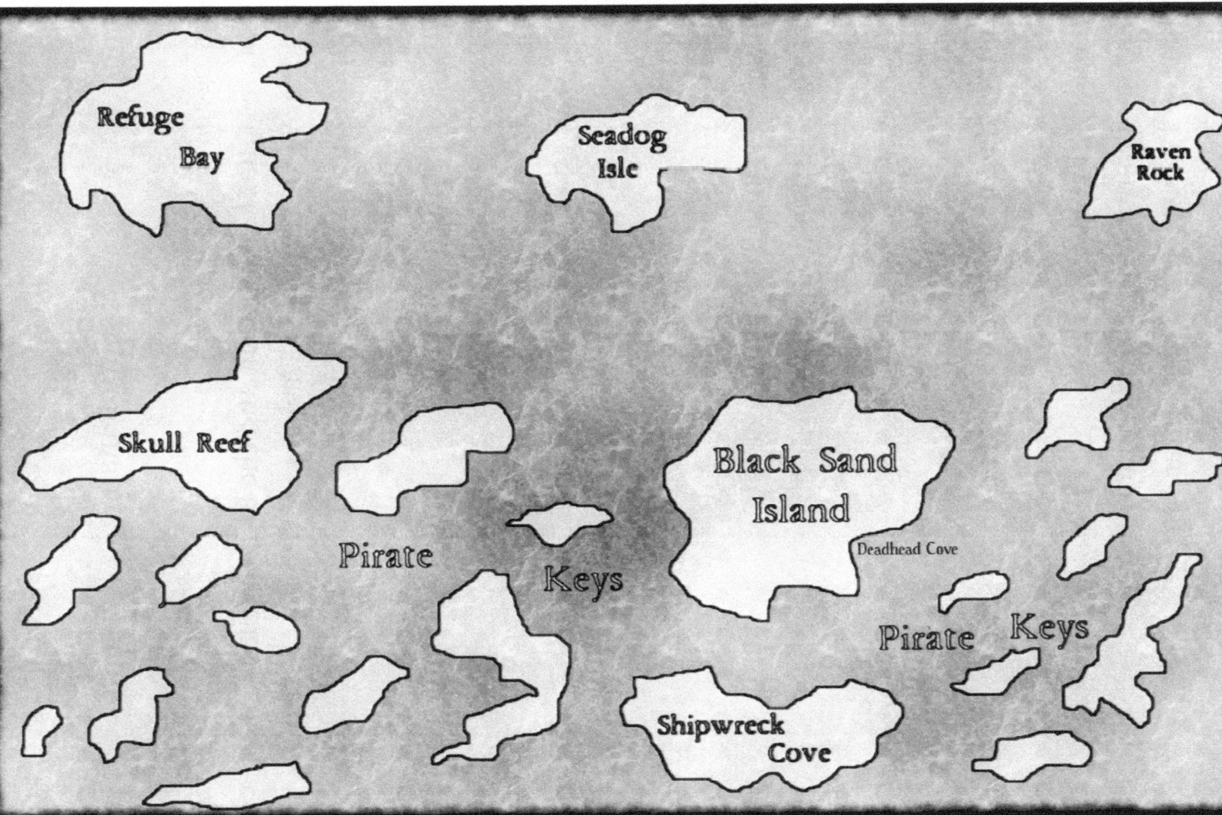

Refuge Bay
Seadog Isle
Raven Rock
Skull Reef
Black Sand Island
Deadhead Cove
Pirate
Keys
Shipwreck Cove
Pirate Keys

Contents

Prologue

Darkness.

The sound of her breath swallowed by silence. Her tranquillity. Then, a flutter of wings echoed in the distance.

She shivered, unexpectedly alarmed. Nothing should be able to trespass in her hallowed place without her knowledge. She stared into the black abyss with a tinge of anger and trepidation. "Is someone there? Reveal yourself! This is my domain, intruder!"

"Calm yourself," a voice replied, with more flapping of wings. "I've come to talk. No more than that, Bevire."

Bevire inhaled sharply at the mention of her name. The darkness shifted, slithering, matching her uneasy mood. "How do you know me? How did you find this place?"

A soft chuckle sounded. "Darkness is my home, Bevire, as it is yours. And you shouldn't whisper secrets to your shadows. Sometimes there are creatures listening."

"Eavesdropping you mean," Bevire snarled, curling her fingers into fists. Around her, the darkness swirled.

"Perhaps a bit. But the darkness and I are friends. Friends sometimes share secrets."

"But I have no secrets," She bit her lip against the lie. "And even if I did, you are not my friend."

"I'd like to be. Wouldn't that be nice? To have a confidant? To be able to share your worries and fears? You have fears, don't you? About those terrible dreams that have been disturbing your slumber?"

"How did you..." She stopped, letting the rest of her admission go unspoken.

"I can feel your fear. The darkness can feel your fear. I want to help. I want to ease your troubles. Talk to me. Confide in me. Let me help you." The voice from the shadows spoke in a soothing, gentle manner like a friend.

Bevire closed her eyes. She wanted to scream, to deny, to send the unknown creature away, but she suddenly felt tired, lost. Alone.

"You are not alone. Not anymore."

"I—I don't—" She wanted to protest, but having someone know, finally know, felt good. She whispered instead. "Yes, I am afraid that...my dreams will come true."

"Ah. My poor dear." More gentle, sympathetic tones and then, "You are wise to fear. Your dreams hold truth. Especially that dread you hold of one particular person." A space of silence fell. Bevire shook in consternation before the voice added. "I can help you with that, help you rid yourself of your fear. Of your enemy."

"An enemy?" Bevire recoiled at her most intimate thought. She lashed out in denial. "I have no enemy! Who do you think threatens me? Tell me!" She shouted her haughty words but knew no lie would hide the secret name in her heart. A name that shouldn't be there. She held her breath as she waited for the voice to speak it aloud.

"Your brother. God of Souls."

A pause, with only her rapid breathing to break the quiet. Then, "I'm listening."

"Excellent. Let me introduce myself. I am the Nightmare Crow."

Shadow on shadow. The fluttering of wings and the even intake of a breath. Bevire and the Crow sat in a circle without form, drawn with the transient substance of night. The Crow sketched runes into the essence of Bevire's sanctuary with a strange ragged claw extended from its foot. She watched his actions, dubious of his intent.

"Are you certain of this?" A frown creased her face. "It seems...unwise."

The crow did not look up from its spell weaving, but answered, nonetheless. "More certain than you know. We bring your brother to his destiny, Goddess of Shadows. What we do here today will change his fate forever..." He paused before continuing. "And protect the gods." A last slash with his claw and the crow stopped his work. He raised his head. "Are you ready?"

"I—I am not sure, this seems..."

The crow clacked his beak. "Do you want your brother to realize his full power? To turn on you as you saw in your dreams?" He reached out and touched a wingtip to her hand. Bevire shook, a sudden wave of fear jolting through her body. The crow ignored her reaction. "This is the one way to stop that. The creature we will awaken will ensure his defeat." He stroked feathers over flesh and Bevire sighed, a slight calm settling over her.

"I want that, but—"

"No doubts." The crow interrupted her objections. "No second thoughts. Be strong, Goddess. You are only protecting your own. He will threaten no god when we are done." The Crow stared at her, his eyes dancing with shadows.

Under his gaze, Bevire took a breath and straightened her back. "You are right. I must be strong. I am ready."

She closed her eyes and summoned her magic. Black night flowed through the runes that the Crow had sketched, lighting them in a dark, pulsing crimson. She chanted, *"Yndreff Und Chryn Llyd. Dwch alyan Und Chryn Llyd.*

Torrych cadwyn. Dy chyd bydri hwn. Yndreff Und Chryn Llyd."

A great burst of crimson light exploded, and the shadows howled. Darkness swirled inside the circle, sweeping away the runes in a vortex that swallowed itself. The crow laughed and Bevire shivered, and below the worlds, an ancient beast stirred.

Chapter One

Lord Merrill and the Shipwreck

The spittle landed on the Black Shoals dock an inch away from Rafe's right foot. He glanced over in annoyance and then glared at the smug smirk of Commander Augustus Quartermain Pelham. Beside the commander, stood a grizzled Navy sailor wiping his mouth with the back of his hand.

Pelham sneered in return. "Well, well, Captain Morrow. Come to slink about town, have you?"

Rafe deliberately stepped on the spittle, smearing it across the weathered wood of the dock. "Commander Pelham. Not a pleasure to see you again. In fact, your presence has entirely blighted this lovely early morning."

"Speak with respect to your betters, scoundrel!" The grizzled sailor was the one to retort, and Rafe moved his attention to Pelham's companion.

The captain gave the man his best stone-faced look. "If I had betters here, I would." Without moving his gaze, he addressed his next question to Pelham. "Who's your elderly friend? He doesn't appear to possess a civil tongue or manners."

"Elderly?" The man in question seemed shocked, and then snapped, "Why you—"

"Be quiet!" Pelham barked, cutting off the rest of the retort, and then addressed Rafe. "My first officer, Captain. Lieutenant Commander Francis Montague. And now that introductions have been made, why don't you toddle off. In fact, feel free to depart the island altogether."

"Is that an order, Commander?" Rafe quirked an eyebrow and dropped a tone of menace in his voice. "Because I don't take orders from the Navy of the Royal Court."

Pelham matched Rafe's antagonism. "Perhaps it's time you started."

Rafe chuckled. "You are an arrogant one. Do you think your superiors would care for you making trouble? Making an enemy of me? Or approve of you chasing trade away from Black Shoals? I'm here on business."

"Business? What business could—"

"Here he comes now." Rafe smiled as he interrupted, pointing to a well-dressed gentleman strolling down the docks.

Commander Pelham turned his head. "Lord Merrill?"

"Yes, I'm transporting some of his goods and the gentleman himself, to Abersythe. He's transferring cargo between his warehouses." Rafe then added with a wider grin, "Perhaps you'd like to tell him personally that you don't want me on Black Shoals."

Rafe watched with glee as the muscles in Pelham's jaw twitched. "No, Captain. That won't be necessary. We'll leave you to your business." After one more glare, the commander stalked off with his first officer.

Lord Merrill arrived in the wake of the commander's retreat. "Was that Pelham? What did that pompous fool want?"

"Nothing of importance. Just his usual bluster."

"I can imagine. The way the man acts, you'd think he runs the entire Navy of the Royal Court. I've seen it before with the Navy elite. They think an appointed commission makes them superior to the enlisted sailors simply because they have an extra insignia. Pelham is one of the worst. I've had many a complaint from my ship captains and administrators here on Black Shoals over his misuse of authority."

"He does like to have his hand in things."

Lord Merrill snorted. "More like meddle. But enough talk of that man. Shall we proceed to your ship, Captain? My cargo should have arrived at your docking berth by now, and I want to supervise its loading."

"By all means." Rafe smiled and motioned with his hand for the lord to go ahead. The pair ambled the docks to the *Celestial Jewel* and boarded the ship. Rafe left his guest in the capable hands of Pinky Jasper and moved to the quarterdeck.

Blackthorne quietly sidled towards Rafe, both men standing above the main deck watching Lord Merrill. The nobleman paraded across the deck, overseeing the loading of his goods, wandering among the crew.

"Are you sure about this, sir? We've never had a proprietor, let alone a nobleman, accompany the cargo before."

"It isn't the usual way of things, but I don't see we have much choice. Our good standing has suffered since the trouble we had with my sister. You know how short we've been of regular cargo runs, and with the lingering ill-will over my actions regarding the portals, temple tithes have been considerably less than usual."

Blackthorne nodded. "Yes sir, that is true. And the Navy of the Royal Court has been none too cordial of late either."

Rafe paused, remembering his recent distasteful encounter. "That, I fear, is our Commander Pelham's doing. I ran into him this morning, and he had the nerve to suggest we had no right to dock here." Rafe paused as he noticed Blackthorne clench his jaw, but continued when the first mate said nothing. "He seemed to want to cause trouble, and we both know he has been bad-mouthing this ship to others. No doubt his campaign against us will persist, and we should expect the Navy of the Royal Court ships to persevere in damaging our reputation." He sighed. "We need money and the good favour from this job."

"I suppose we do." Blackthorne softly sighed. "We are low on supplies. I imagine it won't hurt to have him aboard. He does seem better than most noblemen I've met."

Rafe quirked an eyebrow and suppressed a smile. "No, he isn't quite what I expected, either. He seems less arrogant than some of his peers. He even shares our distaste for Commander Pelham."

"Does he now?" Blackthorne briefly grinned. "Shows the lord has a discerning eye for bad character then if he dislikes that fool."

"Yes, and that may be another reason to cultivate his support. An ally against Pelham might be useful."

Blackthorne gave a nod. "I shall endeavour to do my best, sir."

"Care to test out your resolve? Go help oversee the loading of the cargo and feel out the man. I'd like your opinion."

"Yes, sir." Blackthorne nodded and descended to the lower deck.

Rafe remained, watching his officer's interaction with Lord Merrill. At the ease of their dealings, the knot between his shoulder blades lessened.

This trip might work out to everyone's advantage.

Rafe continued to observe until Lord Merrill's goods had been stowed to his satisfaction and then gave the order for departure. As the ship prepared to leave dock,

Lord Merrill joined Rafe on the quarterdeck.

"How long will we be at sea, Captain? I'm a bit of a novice sailor, I must admit."

"It's about a day's sail, give or take. No need to push the ship with little urgency or perishable cargo."

"Well enough. And just long enough for a pleasurable experience without overstaying my welcome, eh, Captain." Lord Merrill chuckled, and Rafe smiled, the edges of his mouth lifting in genuine amusement.

"I'm sure you'll fit in aboard our ship, milord. You've already put the crew at ease. They're not used to the fine company of nobles, but they've seem to have taken a liking to you."

"Fine praise indeed, as they all appear to be gentlemen of goodly character. Although I must admit, I was a bit apprehensive given the nature of some of your men. Consorting with the dead is not something I've done before." Lord Merrill gave a shake of his head. "Even in my circles, you hear stories about this grand ship, daring feats, and strange adventures. More than a bit off-putting for some, if I may say. I received a few dire warnings when I announced my intentions to sail with you."

"I can imagine, though I suspect many of those tales suffer from exaggeration. I doubt we'll see any adventure on this trip. Most likely we'll have an uneventful voyage.

Several hours out, Rafe's offhanded comment regarding adventure proved to be a terrible prediction indeed.

From high in the rigging came the shout of a sailor. "Dead ahead, Captain! Wrecked ship run aground on Razor Reef!"

In a blink, Rafe grabbed a spyglass and scanned the horizon focusing on the spit of land called Razor Reef. A shudder ran through his blood as he saw a listing ship foundered on its rocks, a gaping hole in the hull.

"Mr. Anders! Starboard turn! Vessel in distress! Hands to the rail! Look for survivors and souls!"

"Aye, aye, sir." Shouts rose in unison with the loud creak of the *Jewel* as Anders turned the wheel. The ship lurched slightly in the waves as she changed course. Rafe hid a smile as Lord Merrill stumbled and grabbed the rail to steady himself.

"Take her in slow, Mr. Anders! We don't want to run aground beside her. Drop the sea anchor off the reef and we'll take a long boat in for a closer look."

Anders grumbled under his breath, and Rafe caught the words, "ain't no green sailor" and "know how to sail," but Anders still gave a nod, followed by an "Aye, Captain." Rafe glanced at Lord Merrill who now seemed two shades paler than a ghoul. He walked over and put a hand on the nobleman's shoulder.

"We're duty bound to give aid to ships in distress, but don't worry. We've navigated this reef before."

Lord Merrill squared his shoulders. "Never had a doubt of it, sir. My sea legs may not be well used, but never let it be said that I shirked duty in those in need of aid."

"Good man."

Lord Merrill straightened his spine under the praise. "I only hope we find survivors."

"Aye to that thought." Rafe stepped away and shouted, "Report! Any sign of crew?"

A chorus of short, negative replies answered and a cry came from Mouse, "Only debris, sir! Not a sign of life or afterlife!"

Rafe sighed.

The ship sailed in as close as it dared, before throwing out the sea anchor and drifting alongside the reef. An unmistakable litter of flotsam floated on the sea, but nary a body. It seemed unnatural and eerie. Muttered prayers drifted on the wind.

"Not that I'm ungrateful, but it seems unusual to find no sailors in the sea after a wreck." The soft voice of Lord Merrill sounded in Rafe's ear underneath the squeals and groans of the winches manoeuvring the longboat into lowering position.

"It is. We usually find survivors or bodies about after a wreck. Perhaps we'll get answers when we visit the shipwreck." Rafe nodded at the longboat now ready for boarding. "If you'll excuse me, I'll be leading the exploration party."

"Of course, Captain. A safe journey."

Rafe nodded and touched his hat in a farewell gesture, before taking his place in the longboat with Striker Angus, Short Davy, and seven more crewmen that included his newest sailors, Red Wilson and Josiah Collins. Stern faces and silence enfolded the journey as they rowed to the shipwreck. They cut through the water as near as they dared, steering past the hole in the hull, none acknowledging the familiarity of the ship prickling their thoughts. They inspected the damage, hoping for signs of survivors clinging to the wreckage or even bodies floating within the cracked interior. They saw nothing but the broken remains of a once proud vessel.

Rafe sighed, his voice solemn. "Take us closer to the bow. I want to see if we can identify which ship this was." He watched them nod, all eyes avoiding his expression.

Only the scrape of the oars and the slap of the waves on the boat sliced the silence of men that followed. Not a grunt nor a whisper sounded as the boat cut through the sea around the strangely abandoned vessel, navigating a better angle to view the faded nameplate upon the bow. The crew avoided staring at the stranded hulk wedged upon the sharp rocks of the reef, most heads looking to the oars or keeping clear of running aground. As they came around, Rafe picked up his spyglass and checked the side of the ship. His heart skipped two beats as he read the name.

"Damnation. It is the *Coral Rose*."

Anguished murmurs and words of prayer finally broke the quiet and Rafe didn't blame his men. The *Coral Rose* was the star in the Abersythe merchant fleet, with many of its sailors known to the crew of the *Jewel*.

"Not one sign of crew? Not living or dea—?"

"Ahoy!" A hoarse shout snapped across the air. "Save me! If you have any decency, I need help!"

All eyes looked to the direction of the desperate voice and there, clutching to the rocks, half hidden by the ship, they saw a sailor. The man raised a hand and feebly waved to catch their attention.

"Ahoy!" Rafe yelled back. "We see you! We're coming!"

He turned to his oarsmen. "Can we get closer to the reef? Close enough to pull him into the boat?"

Striker Angus shook his head. "We can get a wee bit closer, but not near enough to haul him in from where he be positioned."

"I can get him." Josiah Collins stared at Rafe. "Bring the boat in near as you can, and I'll swim out and bring him back." At Rafe's look of doubt, the man added, "I've swum the underwater reefs off Echo Bay. Rescued one or two fools in my day. I know how. Worst we'll get is a few scrapes."

Rafe hesitated, then nodded. "Do it, sailor."

The boat swung in nearer the reef and Collins eased himself into the water. A short swim brought him to the stranded man. With a cry, the frantic sailor launched himself at Collins, grabbing him about the neck like a lifeline. The two went under for a moment, but Collins gave the other sailor a hard smack and fought to the surface with him in tow. The man settled in Collins' grasp, and Rafe's man swam, dragging the poor wretch back to the longboat. Eager hands hauled them back within the safety of the craft. They both rested at the bottom, panting, dripping water onto the weathered wood.

Rafe gave them a smile. "Good job, Collins." His man returned the smile and slowly sat up, leaning against the boat's side. Rafe turned to the rescued sailor. "Are there any more survivors?"

The crewman from the *Coral Rose* shook his head and whispered. "They're all gone. All of them. Don't know how I didn't end up with them. All gone." The sailor curled up, bringing his knees to his chest, and closed his eyes.

Rafe sighed, knowing he'd get no more from the man at present. "Sail us a course about the wreck to make certain and then return to the *Jewel*."

The boat made its route, finding no others, alive or dead, nor souls in need of Rafe's care. They reboarded the *Jewel*, disheartened, but with their passenger more lucid. Lord Merrill was among the first to greet them.

"You found a survivor. Excellent." He snatched a proffered blanket from Blackthorne's hand and wrapped it around the rescued sailor. "Poor lad. What an ordeal you must have gone through."

Rafe tilted his head, a bit surprised at the nobleman's concern, but took advantage. "Why don't you take him below to my quarters, Lord Merrill, and see to his comfort? Davy, escort them down and get them some rum. I'll join you all shortly." Davy nodded and whisked the pair below decks before either could object.

Rafe turned to Blackthorne, giving him and the other crew left aboard the answers to their unspoken questions. "It was the *Coral Rose*. We found no sign of other sailors. Not alive, dead, or spirit."

Hushed quiet settled over the ship, not a word spoken, but mourning on every face. Rafe took a breath before giving his orders. His next words snapped like thunder against twilight.

"Toss a spell orb overboard near the wreck and let the beacon spell stand as a signal warning. Ships that come this way need to know it has been tended upon. Then pull up the sea anchor and set sail back on our original course. We'll give word of the *Coral*'s demise in her home port."

There were nods, and the crew moved to obey, but without cheery banter or any jovial manner. Rafe brushed past them all and went below decks.

He entered his quarters to find Lord Merrill and the rescued sailor both nestled in chairs and sipping on rum. Davy stood quietly in a corner. Rafe nodded at his man who quietly left the room, shutting the door behind him. Rafe moved to his desk noticing that the *Coral Rose* sailor sported some colour in his cheeks and a steadier hand grasped the glass of rum.

As Rafe settled in his chair, Lord Merrill took initial control of the conversation. "The poor lad's name is Simon Reeves, Captain, and he hails from Abersythe. His ship is the *Coral Rose*, although I suspect you know that already." Rafe nodded and Lord Merrill continued. "He's had a shock, of course, but is willing to answer any questions you may have for him. I thought it best you take charge of such inquiries."

"Thank you, Lord Merrill." Rafe smiled and pushed any annoyance at the lord's presumption from his thoughts. He turned to Simon Reeves.

"What happened sailor? How did the *Coral Rose* run aground on Razor Reef? As far as I know, there's been no errant weather and your crew and captain were good sailors. Were you attacked? Was it sea creatures? An assault by pirates?"

The sailor hesitated, chewing on his bottom lip. He downed his remaining rum and took a breath. "You may not believe me, but what I say is the honest truth. Ain't a lie or a story." Reeves took another breath. "It was a wave, sir. Biggest I've ever seen. Taller than half the ship out of the calmest sea you ever saw. Don't know how it came. The sea just heaved. Swamped the ship. Men went overboard, but..." His voice quavered, hesitating to continue.

"But what, sailor?"

"It's like it knew, like a hand guided it. Almost as if the wave came and took 'em. The water sloshed across the deck, aiming like, and took 'em."

"That can't be," The great booming voice of Lord Merrill interjected. "Such a large ship? I never thought..." He stopped talking abruptly and Rafe gave the lord a sideways glance.

Reeves stared into his empty glass. "Told you. Knew you wouldn't believe it."

Rafe cast the sailor some sympathy and turned to Lord Merrill with a look, a mix of scorn and amusement. "We shouldn't talk out of turn, milord. Let him finish. The Outer Islands is full of strange things."

Lord Merrill frowned, but said nothing in reply to the rebuke, simply deferred to Rafe. "Yes, of course. I shouldn't have been so quick to judge." Rafe noticed he gripped the arm of his chair and leaned forward. "Continue your story, Mr. Reeves. My apologies for the interruption."

The shaken sailor stared at the nobleman. "Thank you, sir. I don't blame you for not believing. I'd have said so too, before today. But it ain't a story. I'm telling ya, it ain't. Something's out there. Something bad." He turned his gaze back to Rafe, his body trembling. "The ship just went into the reef after that. I was flung out and swept onto the rocks where you found me."

"It's all right, son." Rafe spoke softly, trying to soothe.

"No, it ain't. Won't ever be all right. Cause it weren't over. More men than me survived the wreck. Survived the wave and being taken by the sea. But—but..." His voice choked and he took a minute to compose himself. "I saw something else, sir. The rest were drowned, sir. Dragged into the depths. Monsters, it was. They came out of the water after the wreck, rising like sea foam. But it wasn't foam. It was bones. The dead coming back from the depths, reaching for the crew. Some didn't even look right, not like men. An awful sight, sir. Awful." Reeves shuddered. "Don't know why they didn't take me." He shook his head. "Don't know why."

Lord Merrill reached out and patted the sailor's knee. "You've been through an ordeal, lad. But be glad you survived and you're here to tell the tale."

"I am, milord. I am. Though I wager few will trust in my story. I can scarce consider it true myself."

"I believe you, Mr. Reeves." Rafe interjected, commanding the attention of the other two. "I've seen things equally as strange, even though your monsters are new to me. You can be assured I'll look into whatever this new threat may be. I'll see you home safely to Abersythe and you can leave the matter in my hands."

"In our hands, Captain." Lord Merrill met Rafe's surprise with a smile. "I'll not be left out of this mystery."

"Sir, I don't think—"

Lord Merrill cut him off with a wave of his hand. "I won't be dissuaded. I meant no offence with my earlier words; I was simply surprised. This is a perplexing mystery. I'll be a part of resolving the matter and that's the end of it. Now, grab yourself a glass and we will all have some of your delightful rum."

Rafe wanted to argue, confused by Lord Merrill's odd change of manner, but a glance at the grateful face of Simon Reeves stopped him. Instead, he found a glass and shared a drink with the other men.

Chapter Two

Lords and Darkness

Rafe stood alone with his thoughts as the ship came in to dock at Abersythe harbour, savouring the view as the early morning sun shone over the town. Reeves' strange story unnerved him, its tragedy shifting in his head, yet in this moment horror and death seemed so distant.

Would it be so wrong to wish it all away?

The thought slipped into his head and a sigh slipped past his lips. What he wouldn't give to ignore the implications of the *Coral Rose*, but he could not.

No, the God of Souls must do his duty.

And there was duty here. In the wee hours of the night he had searched, reached out his senses to the After World. He found crew there from the *Coral Rose*, but not everyone. That meant some had not crossed. Yet, they found no ghosts, no lost spirits in the water. Some crew simply vanished. Rafe leaned against the rail, letting out a breath.

So troubling. Even the eaten leave traces.

And it was bad enough crew members of the Coral Rose were missing. But even more disturbing, he felt faint hints of pain emanating from the After World and a few dark spots he couldn't explore, like black stains hiding his souls. It unbalanced his very sense of being.

How is that even possible?

"Sorry to interrupt, captain." Lord Merrill's voice drifted into Rafe's uneasy musings. "But business needs to be attended regarding my cargo."

Rafe turned, shifting aside his worries for the moment. "Yes, Lord Merrill?"

"I'll be disembarking this morning and returning home. I'd prefer to leave my cargo on board until tomorrow if that's convenient, and I'll send my men along to help with the unloading. There are other things to attend to today, as you know."

"That's fine. It has been a troubling trip."

"It has indeed. More than we bargained for." Lord Merrill hesitated, almost as if he wished to say something else, but only added, "What time shall I send my men?"

"Generally the crew rouses fully by six bells, so between then and eight bells would be best."

"Excellent. I'll send word before they arrive."

Rafe nodded and waited for the man to depart, but Lord Merrill seemed disinclined to leave. Rafe asked, "Was there something else?"

"Yes. The other matters I spoke of, namely Mr. Reeves and the *Coral Rose.*"

Rafe stifled his irritation. Despite his attempts at dissuasion, Lord Merrill continued to insist on taking an interest in the matter. "What about them?"

"I know you plan on taking Mr. Reeves with you when you report to the harbourmaster and relay the sad news of the *Rose's* demise. I shall accompany you. Then I will take Reeves in hand and get him settled back in his home."

Surprised, Rafe stared at the resolute expression on Lord Merrill's face. Then he sighed. "Very well. We depart as soon as the ship is finished docking."

"I shall be ready."

Rafe then watched a satisfied Lord Merrill walk away, before returning his gaze to Abersythe. All feelings of tranquillity had vanished. Around him came the shouts of the crew and the clank of the winches as the heaving lines played out and the mooring crews brought the *Jewel* into port. As the vessel settled in its berth with a familiar bobbing motion and shipboard creaks, Rafe left the quarterdeck to disembark. Lord Merrill and Mr. Reeves awaited him at the top of the gangplank.

"Shall we, Captain?"

Rafe nodded and led the way to the harbourmaster's office.

The docks were bustling with sailors, harbour crew and townsfolk, people starting their workday and others getting their morning meal at the inns and taverns. Men and women wandered past. Laughter drifted out of the dockside pubs, and voices carried from the ships. The carefree, familiar atmosphere eased Rafe's mood, and he felt more in command as he and his two companions entered the harbourmaster's office.

The man looked up from his desk as they crossed the threshold, a smile blossoming on his face. "Captain Morrow. Good to see you, sir. And Lord Merrill. An honour." He rose to welcome them as they approached, extending his hand and craning his neck slightly to look them in the eye. Both Rafe and Lord Merrill shook the harbourmaster's hand, while Simon Reeves simply nodded a greeting. Then all the men took their seats to discuss business.

"I assume you're here to check in and register the unloading of cargo. Will you be offloading this morning or afternoon?"

"Tomorrow morning, Mr. Cooke, but if you pardon, I'd like to defer business for a moment to report sad news." Rafe turned slightly and waved a hand at Reeves. "This gentleman is lately off the *Coral Rose*. I'm sorry to report she's gone aground on Razor Reef, with the loss of all hands save this sailor, Mr. Simon Reeves."

Cooke turned a deathly pale and inhaled sharply. "No! Not the *Rose*! Are you sure?"

"Yes, sir. I saw the ship's name myself when inspecting the wreck."

"And there's no chance of others surviving? Perhaps a longboat? Or floating wreckage." The vain hope the harbourmaster tossed out died when Rafe shook his head. "I see. Did you find any other remnants, Captain? What of uncrossed souls? Were any left behind?"

"No, sir. Not a trace. You see..." Rafe hesitated for a heartbeat and then continued. "The way she went down was a bit beyond the usual manner of things. We didn't witness it, having come across the wrecked ship on our travels. We heard of what happened when we fished poor Mr. Reeves from the sea. He has a story to tell, and you'll want some time to take it in."

"Very well. Tell your tale, Mr. Reeves." Cooke leaned back in his chair, waiting, worry creasing his face.

Both Rafe and Lord Merrill nodded at the sailor, who took a deep breath and told his strange story once more. At the end, Cooke exclaimed, "How horrifying! Are the seas erupting with fresh monsters after only getting rid of the old?" He turned to Rafe. "Have you ever heard of such a thing?"

"No, but I will look into the matter. It may be a creature, or it may be someone doing magic. Either way, it needs to be stopped. As you said, the idea of new terrors in the sea is troubling."

"Most troubling. And the *Coral Rose* their first victim. It is deeply disturbing. And it won't sit well with sailors or the islands. Not so soon after the last adversity. I hope this won't cause you more difficulties, Captain."

"I'll make certain it does not. Captain Morrow is the man to get to the bottom of this calamity." Lord Merrill spoke up, surprising both Rafe and the harbourmaster.

"You've taken an interest, milord?" Cooke inquired, one eye still cast at Rafe.

"Indeed. I'll see to it the mystery is solved and Captain Morrow has all the resources he needs to ferret out the truth."

"That's very generous of you, milord. The people of Abersythe will no doubt appreciate your kindness."

"It is nothing. Those sailors were hard working, decent men and their families deserve to know why they died."

A small mewl from Reeves distracted Lord Merrill and Rafe took the opportunity to interject. "We should send warnings out to the other towns and islands. If some new creature is prowling the seas, ship captains should know."

"Won't do no good," Reeves blurted. "Happens too fast. If it comes, it'll get 'em. Nothing they can do."

Rafe laid a hand on the sailor's arm. "Perhaps. But they should still be warned."

"The captain's right, lad." Lord Merrill spoke softly in a soothing tone. "But you needn't hear this. I'll get you home, and leave the captain and Mr. Cooke to sort out their business." He turned to the harbourmaster. "I'll be seeing to arrangements for a memorial for the *Coral Rose*, so I will be talking to you on this matter again, Mr. Cooke. Very soon." He rose, helping Mr. Reeves to his feet as well. Then he addressed Rafe, "I'll be talking to you soon as well, Captain. Don't believe I won't be in touch. You'll need help in this, I fear."

With a nod farewell, Lord Merrill and Reeves took their leave.

With the close of the door following their departure, Cooke exclaimed, "Extraordinary! The man's clearly taken an interest in you, Captain!"

"So it seems, but why I cannot fathom."

Cooke chuckled. "Don't question your good fortune, sir. Having Lord Merrill on your side is a boon for you, if I may say so." Cooke hesitated and then continued. "You have my support, sir, but as you know, there is much disquiet swirling about you of late. There's been talk, whispers of discontent among the townsfolk and the sailors. And the Navy of the Royal Court has openly been disparaging your reputation. Your ship finding the wreck of the *Rose* will not quell that talk, but the support of Lord Merrill may. The people of Abersythe respect him, and the Navy of the Royal Court will not cross the wishes of a nobleman. You would do well to cultivate his friendship."

"I do not begrudge his support or his friendship, but I worry over how far he will involve himself. This will be dangerous business, Mr. Cooke, and not the sort he should be involved in."

"On that account, ease your fears. Lord Merrill is a canny fellow. On that, you can rely." Cooke smiled briefly, before letting out a small sigh. "Let's get down to business. We both have much to do today."

The hours ticked by and an unsettled day flowed into night, with the crew of the *Jewel* and the people of the town settling into slumber. Over Abersythe, the starlit clouds swirled, and the wind blew past the harbourmaster, past the *Celestial Jewel* wafting far out to sea. The dark waves gently rolled with the shadows bereft of moon while, below the surface, the sea creatures slept to the soft strains of a mother's lullaby.

All seemed serene, yet something in the shadows stirred. Someone emerged from an in-between place, from the blackness of a veiled sanctuary. She swept from the folds of the gloom to a corner of a reef, against the silhouette of the *Coral Rose* shipwreck.

The ruined boat dwarfed her presence, its shade making her uneasy. Its empty shell somehow felt haunted even though it remained bereft of souls. She wondered at the queasy chill in her blood, in her night's shadows even as she repressed the guilt tickling at the back of her mind.

I did this. Her conscience whispered, a persistent itch she tried to deny. *But how could I know? And everything has a price. And what do mortal lives matter to me?*

She turned her gaze away from the ship, staring at the sea. She gathered the night around her like a cloak, reflexively trying to hide. Above her head, she heard the beat of wings and the caw of a crow. The bird swooped down out of the sky and landed at her feet.

She stepped back, startled, and snapped at the creature. "Why did you want to meet here? Of all places?"

The Nightmare Crow cackled. "Why, Bevire, so testy you are. Are we having regrets so soon?"

"No! Of course not!" Harsh denial slipped from her lips, wrapped in anger that the Crow's words hit so close to her thoughts. "But I don't see why you dragged me to the mortal world." Her peripheral vision caught a glimpse of the *Rose*. "I hate it here."

The Crow chuckled. "Such a bad liar, but no matter. What's done is done." He moved a few steps, toward the shipwreck. "Such a carcass it makes, this ship. Such a statement. That's why I asked to meet here. I thought you might want to see what we've wrought."

"Bah!" Bevire turned away, her breathing suddenly rapid. "What do I care of some wrecked ship and dead mortals? I did not want this! These—these..." She stumbled over her words, finally spitting out, "Distractions and delays." She whirled around glaring down at the crow. "You said working the spell you gave me would rid this world of the threat my brother posed! And the threat he poses to me and my family! That's what I want! Nothing else!"

"Such impatience. You must learn to play the long game, Goddess. The spell will do its work, in time." The crow took a small step. "First we need to strengthen the beast that we summoned to challenge your brother."

"With ships of foolish mortals? You waste my time, creature!" Her shadows violently shifted. "I did not agree to this! To playing games!" The pitch of her voice rose to a shriek and her eyes flashed black. "All I wanted was the threat of my brother removed!"

The crow flapped his wings and clacked his beak. "Calm yourself, Bevire. These things are intricate. Beasts of this power need to be awakened slowly. You must—"

"I must do nothing!" With a scream of rage, fuelled by guilt, Bevire kicked the Nightmare Crow, sending the bird flying across the rocky reef. The crow rolled with an infuriated squawk and a trail of feathers before leaping to the sky on his wings.

"How dare you strike me! How dare you!" His voiced screeched, the air around him quivering.

"I dare, remnant! I am the Goddess of Night and Shadows! Of Darkness itself! I am no mad goddess waiting on your pleasure!" She laughed, taking delight in the Crow's momentary surprise at her knowledge. It hadn't been hard to deduce his involvement with the Goddess of the Moon. She lifted her chin, a haughty expression on her face. "I will not be so easily swayed as my sister. Tell me how long I need to wait for my brother's ruin or fly off and lick your wounds, Nightmare Crow!"

The bird flew circles around the reef, angry, shrieking caws filling the air. He finally settled on a rock facing Bevire and fluffed his feathers. "I do not like demands. Nor kicks. I will not forget this insult."

"I don't care. Tell me what I want to know."

"I cannot. I do not know myself."

"What?" Bevire stepped towards the Nightmare Crow, her darkness surging, blotting out the stars and clouds. The reef suddenly plunged into obsidian night. "Explain yourself, Crow! What did you make me do?"

"What I needed you to do, of course." It was the crow's

turn to laugh. "You played your part magnificently, oh Goddess, so willing to guard the world against the supposed threat of your brother."

"Supposed threat?" The goddess felt her gut churn. "What of my dreams? They foretold of his menace. Prophesized it."

The Crow chuckled. "Who can say where dreams come from? Your own subconscious fears? Happenstance? And yes, sometimes a prophecy. Sometimes, though, they fly on dark wings." The crow fluttered his own wings.

Bevire gasped. "It was you? You sent the dreams?"

The Crow tilted his head. "Does it matter? You wanted to believe. That was enough."

She took a step back, her darkness whirling around her, a hand pressed against her chest. "What have I done?" Guilt and horror rushed through her blood. "What did you make me do?"

"I made you do nothing! You were quite willing. And I never lied to you. The spell I gave you will indeed summon an ancient beast powerful enough to destroy the brother you fear so much. Just not as you convinced yourself." The Crow chuckled. "You never asked the right questions, Goddess. You rarely doubted any of my words, nor asked my motives. You never even asked yourself what kind of a thing could destroy a god. Or whether that power could be contained."

Bevire trembled slightly, and her voice whispered. "What do you mean?"

The crow stretched his wings. "Did you actually think such a thing was simply slumbering benevolently under the sea? It was imprisoned, you fool. Locked away to protect this world from its insatiable hunger."

Bevire gasped and the crow hissed in glee.

"For now it is weak, drained from years of being deprived of its true power. I do not know how long it needs to rise nor do I know exactly what it will do when fully awake. I do know it lives to destroy and that will be enough. Your brother will try to stop it, stop its servants, and the devastation it will cause. The great Rafe Morrow will step right into its path, and then..." The crow gave a harsh shriek, and the goddess jumped. "Then, Bevire, we will have what I want. The beginning of the end and the God of Souls right where I need him to be." With a laugh, the Nightmare Crow sprang into the air and flew from Bevire's sight.

She shivered, her shadows retreating, leaving her shaking under a starlit night. Behind her, the creaking silhouette of the *Coral Rose* loomed.

Chapter Three

Costs

Morning came with familiarity and the unloading of Lord Merrill's cargo. Crates of fabric, of rum, of furniture and other goods, were off-loaded on to wagons destined for a dockside warehouse. Rafe stood on the quarterdeck watching the bustling scene. Well-known footsteps sounded behind him. Rafe exhaled.

"What is it, Blackthorne?"

The first mate moved into view, standing beside him at the rail. "Lord Merrill has arrived, sir."

"I saw. Interesting that he's come personally to oversee the unloading of his cargo. But you hardly had to announce his presence."

"He isn't here for the cargo, sir. He's requested permission to come aboard."

"Has he now? Our lord is persistent, I'll give him that. Escort him aboard, and I'll see you both in my quarters."

Both men walked down to the main deck where Blackthorne veered off to fetch Lord Merrill, and Rafe continued below decks to his quarters. He retrieved a small bottle of berry cordial from his cabinet and three glasses.

Then he put them on his desk, sat in his chair, and waited. A few moments later, a knock came at the door.

"Enter."

A click of the latch, and both Blackthorne and Lord Merrill moved into the cabin, closing the door behind them. The two men sat down, and Rafe nodded a greeting to his guest.

"Good morning, Lord Merrill. What can I do for you today?" He reached over and picked up the bottle. "Cordial?"

"Ah, sweet berry I see. A delight. I'd love a glass."

Rafe poured three glasses, each man picking up their drink and settling into their chair with a sip.

"First rate cordial, sir. I appreciate the hospitality." Lord Merrill smiled. "And as I think you already suspect, I'm here about the dreadful business of the *Coral Rose* and to offer you a proposition."

Rafe raised an eyebrow, surprised. "A proposition, milord?"

"Indeed. I shall be blunt, Captain. It is no secret that recent events have left your good name somewhat sullied. And the tactless efforts of Commander Pelham to further tarnish you and your crew have left you all at a disadvantage. Without the goodwill of the people, you will be hampered in your endeavours to find out what happened to the *Coral Rose*. I dare say Commander Pelham may even try to lay blame on you for the tragedy."

Blackthorne snorted. "It would be like Pelham to try such a dirty trick." He sipped his drink and added, "Sir. Milord." He nodded at his companions. Lord Merrill chuckled, and Rafe suppressed a smile.

"Regardless of any supposition and my first mate's opinion, you are not wrong in your assessment of the situation. What are you suggesting I do?"

"Allow me to offer a certain amount of protection. Let me put out the word that I have engaged you to investigate the attack on the *Coral Rose*. If you are seen under my banner, so to speak, it will, at the very least, keep the interference of the Navy of the Royal Court at bay."

Rafe set his glass down and leaned back in his chair. He studied the lord for a moment, gauging whether to trust him. He glanced at Blackthorne, who seemed eager to say something.

"What do you think of this proposal, Blackthorne?"

"That I'd sooner trust Lord Merrill than Pelham, sir. And I can't see how we would be harmed by accepting his generous offer. Quite the opposite, in fact. There's talk around the docks already this morning, and it does not favour us, Captain. If we leave it lie, I fear it will simply get worse."

Unease quivered along his thoughts. Blackthorne was right, but still. Rafe sighed. "Since you've been blunt with me Lord Merrill, I shall be equally so with you. I have no objection to your support or your protection in the matter of my reputation. On that front, I am grateful and would accept your offer. I do hesitate, though, on how far you wish to be involved in finding the truth on what happened to the *Coral Rose*. Discovering the facts will be no lark or adventure, but most likely a dangerous quest."

"Rest easy your apprehension, Captain. I have no wish to go there. I leave all such troubles in your capable hands. My only wish is to see you accomplish the task of determining the truth and protecting the Outer Islands."

Rafe lightly traced the edge of his desk with a finger. "How would this alliance work, then? This flying under your banner?"

"Leave that business to me. All you need to concern yourself with is finding out what new menace is threatening us. All I'll need are updates of your progress. Just send me word from time to time and any need you may have of my resources." Lord Merrill smiled and sipped the last of his cordial. "Command your ship, sir, as you always have, and, with my aid, you'll find easier harbours and a friendlier welcome." He placed his empty glass on Rafe's desk and held out a hand. "Do we have an accord?"

Rafe took a breath and shook the man's hand. "We do."

"Excellent. I'll take my leave, then. I'm sure you gentlemen have much to discuss. I can show myself off the ship." He rose and tipped his hat. "Good day to you both."

With another smile, Lord Merrill left Rafe's quarters.

"Well, Blackthorne, for better or for worse we have a new ally. I only hope we can trust him."

"Time will tell, sir, but by my reckoning, we don't have better choices. And if it goes rotten, we'll handle it, as always." Blackthorne shrugged. "Maybe good fortune has blown our way this time."

"Perhaps. I just hope I haven't done something we'll all regret."

✳

After the departure of Lord Merrill and the off-loading of his cargo, Rafe went ashore with the late morning sun at his back. He made a few stops, one of which included a visit to the bank to check on Lord Merrill's payment, and visited his suppliers to order more provisions for his ship. Passersby cast fearful or even angry glances his way, though not a one spoke to him.

On completion of his last errand, Rafe made his way from the harbourside, past the town limits, to a narrow trail along the seashore that few bothered to follow. He walked the path with the wind gently blowing and the tang of salt sea in the air until, at last, he arrived at a small stone cottage. He moved towards its sturdy wooden door and knocked. Inside, he heard a yelp, a banging noise, and then a flurry of footsteps. The door yanked open and a tall bespectacled man appeared, greeting him with a, "Yes, what is it?" and then, "Oh, my, Captain Morrow! Come in, come in." The man stood aside, sweeping his arm, and

Rafe entered the cottage. He noticed a dishevelled pile of books on the floor and smiled.

"Good to see you again, Evan. Did you drop your books again?" Rafe nodded to the pile on the floor. For such a brilliant scholar, the poor man was quite uncoordinated at times.

Evan shut the door and replied, "I'm afraid so. Your knock startled me. I don't receive many visitors and the ones I do tend to be either of the annoying sort or students come for a tutoring lesson." He hurried to the mess and bent down. "I'll have this cleared in a moment. Have a seat."

Rafe settled on a hard, wooden chair, elbow resting on the small matching table and watched Evan retrieve his books and neatly stack them on a bookshelf, one of many that lined the walls of the room and that, Rafe knew, filled the rest of the cottage. The only other furniture in this sitting area—a wooden armchair and a writing desk—were also covered in books as well as sheaves of ink-stained paper. With his tomes tucked back into place, Evan turned to Rafe.

"Care for some tea? I have a lovely blend from Shadow Cay."

"No, thank you. I can't stay long. Have a seat, Evan. I need to discuss an important matter."

"Oh dear, that doesn't sound good." Evan pulled at his chair and flopped down onto the seat, a worried expression on his face. "Your important matters generally involve dangerous things like witches and pirates and things that want to eat you. What horrible creature is it now?"

"I don't know. That's why I came to you. I thought perhaps you might be able to help me with some research, either from your private collection or the Abersythe History Guild."

"You don't know?" Evan straightened his spine, his voice laced with incredulity. "You, God of Souls, centuries old, don't know what creature he hunts?" Evan drew in a breath. "Tell me what happened. Are we all doomed?"

Rafe smiled, despite the seriousness of his visit. "I hope not. Have you heard the news about the *Coral Rose*?"

Evan shook his head.

"She wrecked on Razor Reef, but the lone survivor of the crew had an odd story to impart. He said the ship was swamped by a giant wave, sweeping men overboard to their doom. Once the ship ran aground on the rocks, the remaining men were dragged under by bones."

Evan sucked in a breath. "Bones?" He frowned, his attention distracted. "Are you sure it was bones? As in dead men? Skeletons?"

"He didn't say exactly, but I believe that was his meaning, yes. Does that ring a bell, Evan? Do you know something?"

"I may. It might be nothing, but recently I was commissioned to do a bit of research—Wait." He held up a hand and leapt to his feet. "It would probably be best to show you. Give me a moment." Then he rushed from the room, to return a few minutes later with an open book in his hand. "Here it is." He placed the book down in front of Rafe. "*Creighton's Book of Monsters*. There is a small section, starting with this passage." He tapped a page. "It's an old poem, a warning not to inter a man at sea. It may be the basis of the old sailor's legend. You know the one, that superstition some sailors have about sea burial."

Rafe pulled the book closer, and read the passage:

Below the light,
Asleep in the night,
Ashetus waits for the drowned.
The dead he collects,
their bones will protect,
Ashetus, their lord and master.

Cast not the dead,
down to the sea,
Lest they rise to serve Ashetus.
Please give them their rest,
Not under the sea.
Oh, let their dead bones be.

"It does seem similar to the tales I've heard from sailors and sea burial, but who is this Ashetus? I've never heard of such a being."

"I don't know much myself, but I think he is mentioned in a few *very* old legends, where he was depicted as a vicious sea monster or something similar. This book is just a collection of bits and pieces. I'm not even certain how much is accurate. But turn the page. There is an illustration."

Rafe flipped the page to see a drawing of a great beast with a bulbous head, six eyes, a long body ending in a fish tail, and ten tentacles. It also had a great, round mouth full of sharp teeth.

"It looks like a cross between the Kraken and a Sea Wyrm. But what does this Ashetus legend have to do with the bones of dead men drowning sailors and wrecking ships?"

"According to another passage in the book, supposedly from a scrap of an ancient legend, this sea creature keeps the bones of those who are buried at sea as his servants. He sends them out to find living people and drown them, bringing back the corpses for him to eat."

"Well, he sounds like a delightful fellow." Rafe closed the book with a thud and set it on the table. "It doesn't seem very credible, though, that this—this forgotten beast has somehow, suddenly reappeared? Bones and skeletons notwithstanding."

"True. But it is an odd coincidence. And that's not all. You know I keep my ear to the ground, and, lately, I've hearing of a few odd stories about the dead rising from the depths. Normally, I wouldn't pay heed, but with my commission, I've been wondering if..." He let the rest of his sentence hang. "Things feel so strange lately. A few months ago, the events with the Moon Goddess wouldn't have seemed credible, or possible."

"But—but..." Rafe stopped talking, his thoughts churning. He wanted to say that it was impossible, but Evan could be right. Such a word might not apply these days. He stared at his friend. "Who hired you, Evan? To do your research?"

Evan picked up his book, hugging the volume to his chest, and ignored Rafe's question. "Maybe I'm wrong. Reading into things. You know I do that sometimes. Maybe it's not so terrible, maybe it's simply someone using magic, resurrecting the dead. It just seemed so similar." He tried to sound reassuring but failed.

"You didn't answer me, Evan." Rafe pressed the issue, sure his friend was hiding something. "Perhaps, you are wrong, but we can't discount the possibility there is a connection. Who hired you?"

"I—I can't..." Evan hesitated, reluctant to speak. "What I know, it's not...I can't. But the source of this information, where I was told to look, that stems from the Society of the Shadow Guard."

"That old magic guild?" In his surprise, Rafe let Evan's vague answer go unchallenged.

"Yes, but not just old. They still exist today. They like to preserve ancient lore." Evan chewed on his lip. "They also like to keep their secrets."

"A bit like you." Rafe frowned, with still a hint of question and confrontation in his words.

"Perhaps." Evan took a step back. "I could say much the same of you."

Rafe sighed, studying Evan's face. He knew his friend well enough to realize he would not reveal any names. So

Rafe only added, "I need to know more about this Ashetus. Do you have any more information on him?"

Evan shook his head. "I just found the one book and very little in that. But you could try Red Bay on Crickwell Island. The old museum and library there have an extensive collection of archaic books on island folklore. I've been trying to get a look at it for years, but can't get an invitation." Evan sighed and Rafe heard the envy in his voice. "They may open their doors for you, though."

They may indeed. Lord Merrill might be able to help with that as well.

Rafe smiled and nodded his thanks. "I appreciate the help, Evan. I'll take my leave now." Rafe rose, but Evan touched his arm.

"It was good to see you again. I'm sorry I couldn't help more." Evan withdrew his hand from Rafe's arm. "Just be careful. I hope we're wrong, but if not, good luck, old friend."

"Thank you." Rafe turned still wondering what Evan wasn't telling him and left the cottage. He headed back down the path to Abersythe and his ship.

On his return to the harbour a short time later—after a quick stop to send a message to Lord Merrill—the unpleasant sight of the Navy of the Royal Court ship, *The Sea's Favour*, greeted him. He scowled at the vessel, Pelham's ship, only two berths over from the *Jewel*. Waiting on the dock, blocking his way to the *Celestial Jewel*, stood the commander. Rafe sighed and veered left, making to skirt around the unpleasant naval officer, but Pelham moved with him, deliberately getting in his way, obviously spoiling for a confrontation. Rafe glared, grinding his teeth, and stopped. If Pelham wanted words, he'd oblige.

"Kindly get out of my way, Pelham. I don't have time for your bullying nonsense today."

Rafe's aggressive stance seemed to startle Pelham,

but he recovered quickly. "I've come to warn you, Captain. To stay far away from the matter of the *Coral Rose*. The Royal Navy will be salvaging her and dealing with that preposterous story told by that sailor Reeves. He's obviously lying, and I aim to bring him in and have the truth from him." Pelham sneered. "And I want you out of Abersythe when I do. There'll be none of your nonsense or interference."

Rafe smiled, a grin almost as wide as the sea itself. "Lord Merrill might have something to say about your plans, Commander." He spoke softly, his voice full of amusement. "Merrill has taken charge of Reeves and his care, and he won't be pleased with your plans to question him. Nor will he care for your useless orders to keep me away from the *Coral Rose* tragedy. In fact, he's commissioned me to look into the matter." Rafe leaned forward, adding a touch of menace to his voice. "So take your pompous pronouncements and choke on your words, Commander. I'm quite tired of your vendetta."

The look of outrage and shock on Pelham's face made any misgivings Rafe felt over his bargain with Merrill vanish in a burst of smug satisfaction. The captain chuckled as Pelham's face flushed red, but his laughter broke at Pelham's burst of temper.

"Why you, sea snake!" Screaming like a madman, Pelham took a swing at Rafe, but his fist hit empty air as Rafe dodged. The captain stuck out his foot and Commander Pelham went facedown onto the docks, landing with a thud on the old wood.

"Stay down, Commander." Rafe cautioned. "Everyone is watching and you are dangerously close to overstepping your naval authority. Right now we can leave this between us, but if you get up, it will not end well for you."

Rafe watched Pelham curl the fingers of his right hand into a fist, but the commander replied, "You win this round, Captain Morrow, but don't think this is over."

"Of course not, Pelham, you haven't the sense for that."
Rafe turned on his heel and walked to his ship, whistling an old sea shanty.

Chapter Four

Dreams and Bones

In the dark void, she sat, cross-legged, her eyes closed. Old words whispered from her tongue, words taught to her by her father, Reis, Sovereign of the Gods. Spells to pierce the veil between realms, to gain sight beyond worlds, beyond gods, beyond time. In her home, her sanctuary, Bevire used those words to find a power older than the Seven Kingdoms and the Outer Islands, older than the After World and her family, as old as the creatures dwelling in the Archipelago of Nightfall.

She sought answers to questions she never asked.

She sought the beast she had awakened.

Around her, the shadows shimmered, slowly parting inch by inch, swirling down into the sea. In her mind, she followed, sinking below the waves, past her sister Lynna's realm, past the site where Manume's children slept. Falling, sinking deeper into the dark, into the cold, out of the mortal world into a hidden place that even the sea itself refused to name.

And there she saw it. The great beast. A gasp escaped her disembodied lips, and it turned its head. It stared at her with six red eyes.

A screeching caw snapped the vision and she open her eyes to the black of her home. She heard the flap of wings and a voice. The Nightmare Crow.

"Naughty, naughty. Shouldn't spy on Ashetus. Leave it be, Goddess. What's done is done."

"Not yet!" Bevire reached out into her darkness towards the Crow.

Rafe awoke with a start, the dream jolting him from his sleep. His heart raced and his breath came fast. He could feel the fear in his blood and his magic lit his sleeping quarters in a soft blue radiance. He closed his eyes and calmed himself, slowing his breathing, letting his power fade. But the faint images of the unsettling dream remained.

Six red eyes and darkness...and a woman. Someone familiar, but I can't...can't remember.

He tried to hold on to the visions, but they faded out like morning fog meeting the midday sun, shadows of what he originally experienced. Only the fear remained, and the persistent thought that death was rising to feast on the Outer Islands. He took another breath to steady his nerves and threw off the bedcovers.

No sense trying to sleep now.

Rafe dressed, unsteady fingers buttoning his shirt and jacket, and walked out on the deck. A few of the crew were sprawled on the main deck, sleeping under the stars. He quietly manoeuvred his way around the men and climbed to the quarterdeck. He came upon Mouse who stood by the rail, staring at the harbour. The lad jumped back, a guilty look plastered across his face.

"Begging your pardon, Captain. I know I shouldn't be up here—"

"At ease, sailor." Rafe cut off Mouse's apology. "No

need to explain. It's the best view on the ship, especially at night." Rafe glanced out at the town. "Abersythe looks so peaceful, doesn't it? With just a scattering of lights flickering in the darkness."

"Aye, sir. Like little beacons of warmth. Of home."

Rafe leaned against the rail next to his crewman. "Do you miss it, being ashore, being one of the living?"

"Sometimes, but being dead on this ship ain't that different. And I have friends, a place to belong. Never had that alive." Mouse sighed. "I do miss the taste of stewed pie though. My Granny made one that would melt in your mouth and warm your gullet. I miss that, I sure do."

Rafe smiled, and some of his tension eased. "It sounds like something worth missing."

"It is, sir." Mouse fell silent and then blurted, "Are we in for it again, sir? Crew's been talking. Finding the *Rose* unsettled us."

Rafe ran a finger along the wood of the rail. "I believe we are, Mouse. I hope I'm wrong, but something terrible may be coming." Rafe watched the lad shiver and added. "No use worrying about it tonight. We both should get some sleep. Provisions will be arriving in the morning to load and we'll be setting sail for Crickwell Island soon."

Rafe patted Mouse on the shoulder and returned below decks.

❖

The following morning, Rafe stifled a yawn as he listened to Blackthorne. Despite his words to Mouse, further sleep had eluded him.

"The ship's stores arrived and are now all stowed in the hold despite the grumblings of the dock crew and the delivery men. The looks I received overseeing the shipment...I wanted to box the ears of every one of them! And two of our men were turned away at the *Jolly Dog* where they've been drinking for two years. The town's blaming us for the *Coral Rose*. You should hear some of the nonsense floating about. So much for Lord Merrill's supposed influence."

"Give him time, Blackthorne. You can't expect attitudes to change all at once. Besides, Pelham and his lot are in town. No doubt they're responsible for stirring up the rumours. After our altercation, he's likely more determined to smear our good name."

"I heard about that." Blackthorne smiled. "I wish I had seen him fall on his face. The man represents all that's wrong with the Navy of the Royal Court."

"That was his own fault. He did not take the news about Lord Merrill's support well."

"Something good came out of our alliance then."

"More than one thing. Merrill got my message and sent one this morning in return. He sent word ahead to the Red Bay museum. They should be expecting us. Are we ready to set sail to Crickwell Island?"

"Yes, sir. I think the harbour crews will be well glad to be rid of us." Blackthorne pursed his lips, but continued, "What do we hope to find there, sir? An odd place to go looking for monsters or magic, if I may say."

"Not if the thing we're looking for has been forgotten by most and only a remnant is left in legends and stories." Rafe leaned forward. "Do you know the old sailors' tale? The superstition of burying the dead at sea?"

"Vaguely, sir."

"Apparently it's based on an old tale, Blackthorne, one that tells of a beast living far deep under the sea. A creature that feeds on the flesh of drowned corpses. And when the bodies are picked clean, it resurrects their bones to attend its needs."

"A gruesome fable. Is that what we're dealing with? Some forgotten monster come to life? Do you think the story is true?"

"I don't know. I've never heard of this story, save

for the old superstition. I mean, Lynna rules the sea and she's never heard nor seen such a creature." Rafe paused, glancing at Blackthorne who stared back with a look of consternation. "Yet, now I wonder. What if it exists? If there is a beast so ancient, so powerful that it can hide from the gods?"

"That is a troubling thought."

"Indeed. That's why we sail to Red Bay. We need to know more of this beast, whether we're chasing foolish whims or something monstrous." Rafe closed his eyes, grim thoughts dashing around his head.

"Are we heading out straight away, sir?" Blackthorne's voice pulled his attention back. "Lord Merrill is holding his memorial for the Coral Rose crew this afternoon. He's asked us to be in port."

Rafe opened his eyes, a frown on his face. "Is that wise, given the current state of things?"

"Perhaps not, but our men knew the crew of the *Rose* and have as much right to pay their respects and say their farewells as anyone. We've done nothing wrong. We shouldn't have to slink around and hide." He paused then added, "I don't think any Navy of the Royal Court sailors will be there."

Rafe raised an eyebrow. "Why do you say that?"

"Navy ships went out this morning, though not Pelham's, damn the luck. Word is, they are salvaging the *Coral Rose*. If they can't repair her enough to bring the ship home, they'll recover her goods and sink her. The *Sea's Favour* is the only Navy ship left in port, and I don't see Lord Merrill extending an invitation to that crew."

Rafe pursed his lips, his better judgment telling him to refuse permission, but then let out a sigh. "Any man wanting to pay his respects can go."

"I think the men will be glad to hear it." Blackthorne tilted his head. "Will you be going, sir? The men will expect it."

"I know." Another sigh. "I'll make an appearance at least, but if there's ill will I won't stay."

"Fair enough, sir." Blackthorne lowered his head for a moment, before giving Rafe a hard stare. "There's something else, isn't there, sir? Something that kept you up last night?"

Rafe blinked, a bit taken aback at his first officer's direct question. "You should have been a spy, Blackthorne. No secrets are safe around you."

Blackthorne grinned. "Can't help it, sir, if I'm excellent at my duty."

"That you are, and you are correct. There is something else. I had a dream, a vision, perhaps. Images and thoughts I can't quite recollect save for red eyes, fear, and the certainty that death is coming for us."

"That doesn't bode well. Will we be sailing to see the new Oracle? After Red Bay? If you're having visions?"

Rafe shook his head. "Not yet."

Blackthorne rose to his feet, waiting to be dismissed. "If that's all, Captain, I'll return topside and inform the crew about the memorial."

"Not quite, Blackthorne. I'd like to know what you aren't telling me." Rafe smiled at the flicker of surprise on his first mate's face. "You accepted my tales of ancient beasts and superstitions too readily. Even for you. Why?"

"Well, sir, on this ship I would never discount the possibility of anything." Rafe chuckled as Blackthorne continued. "And I've heard similar talk around the docks since we put into port. Reeves' tale has gotten out, and some have said they've seen similar things. Fishermen and sailors saying that they've encountered strange waves heaving out of the sea and then disappearing. Waves topped with a peculiar looking sea foam. One man claims he saw a skeletal hand rise from one of the waves. I wasn't sure what to make of it, whether these stories were true or just parroted talk. But it could be that the *Coral Rose* wasn't the first incident."

"Damnation. Evan said something similar during our visit." Rafe scowled. "This may be worse than we feared."

After midday, Rafe and his men gathered for the memorial with the crowd in the town square. The captain's mood was brittle and he expected trouble, but aside from a few sour glances and muttered grumbles, the crew of the *Celestial Jewel* were left alone.

The townsfolk erected a shrine in a secluded section of the square, and Rafe watched men, women, and children place offerings beside the stone. An array of flowers, trinkets, and luck charms soon surrounded the monument, as well as a few sweets and personal mementos of the lost sailors. He held his breath as Blackthorne placed a traditional sea wreath of white wildblooms at the shrine. No one said a word. As the last person laid their gift, Lord Merrill moved to the front of the crowd to speak, and Rafe began to relax. The nobleman caught the captain's eye and gave a nod before starting his speech.

"We are here to mourn the loss of those brave and gallant men who perished in the tragic sinking of that fine ship, the *Coral Rose*." Merrill paused a moment with a slight intake of breath. "Abersythe took pride in her and her crew, and they always did us proud. I know not a soul in this town who won't feel their loss, and, for some, it will be a terrible personal tragedy." Lord Merrill lowered his head in a brief moment of silence, and the crowd hushed as well. Then he looked up, casting a poignant gaze over the crowd. "But we will persevere. It is the way of the Islands." He nodded and stepped aside making way for Mr. Cooke, the harbourmaster.

"Thank you, Lord Merrill. It is a sad day and a sad loss for Abersythe. I knew the captain of the *Coral Rose* as a friend and as a fine, honourable man. I feel his passing keenly as many of you here, kin to the crew, feel a similar loss." A breath caught in his throat before he continued. "Today we gather here to mourn and to remember. Remember the captain and all those fine men and women who sailed on our *Coral Rose*." Mr. Cooke straightened his shoulders and lifted his chin. "To the *Coral Rose*. Long may she sail in the After World!"

Rafe shivered at those words, knowing how many of the crew were missing from the After World. His gut churned in guilt as voices rose from the gathering in echo of the harbourmaster's sentiment.

"To the *Coral Rose*."

Rafe saw a hint of a cheerless smile cross the harbourmaster's face as he finished his speech. "And now, anyone who would like to come and say a few words about the *Rose* are welcome." Mr. Cooke merged into the crowd as people walked forward.

As the crowd shifted, Rafe slowly departed the town square. He was more than willing to leave and his crew could maintain a continued presence for the *Jewel* at the memorial. He did not intend to overstay his welcome and tempt goodwill, but, unfortunately, his surreptitious exit did not go unnoticed. At the edge of the square, Rafe found himself impeded.

"Well, well. Captain Morrow." Pelham's voice boisterously rang out, drawing attention. "Leaving so soon? Or simply turning tail and running like a coward? Knowing full well the good people of Abersythe don't want you here." The commander sneered. "After all, where you go trouble follows...like the trouble that found the *Coral Rose*."

A heated murmur snaked through the crowd at Rafe's back. He could almost feel the sudden antagonism build in the crowd as Pelham's insinuation stirred the embers of old resentments. He stepped forward to make a hasty exodus, but Pelham deliberately hindered him.

The commander leaned in, his voice low. "Look around you, Captain. See the people turn on you. Your influence is ending as will soon end these ridiculous adventures of yours."

Rafe glared, sharply ready for a fight, but a flurry of movement behind him gained the fast attention of everyone.

"You're not welcome here!" The harsh shout of the Abersythe harbourmaster rose above the hum of the crowd. "Not after what you've done!"

Shocked, Rafe turned, expecting the anger directed at him, but saw Mr. Cooke staring at Pelham.

"I got word from a spellcaster before I came, from the Black Shoals harbourmaster. Told me the Navy ain't just trying to salvage the *Rose*. They're planning on taking her and her cargo, if they're able, to the King's Rock Fort! And if they have to scuttle her, they'll still take her goods! They're confiscating her! A lawful Abersythe ship! For investigatory purposes, they're claiming! More like for thievery!" He almost snarled the last few words. "So turn around, Commander Pelham, and get your backside gone from this memorial! And don't go besmirching the captain here. Whatever he's done, or ain't done, he's always protected us, been on our side! More than you can say!"

Pelham stepped forward as if to challenge, but the crowd's mood had, yet again, turned, this time against the commander. People now glared at the Navy man, shouting angry insults and waving fists. Cries of "How dare they take the *Rose*!," "It's our ship!," "Navy curs!," "Damn kingdom arrogance!," and "Run him out of town!" drowned any argument, and convinced Pelham to beat a hasty retreat with his men at his heels.

Rafe watched Pelham's withdrawal with amusement but whispered to Blackthorne who had appeared at his side. "I think we should leave as well before they remember any grievance towards us."

Blackthorne nodded. They rounded up crew of the *Celestial Jewel* and quietly left the square, returning to the harbour and their ship.

Once on board, Rafe smiled and let out a sigh of relief. "Well, Pelham's put his foot in it this time. Abersythe won't soon forget this."

"Good." Blackthorne chimed in. "He won't get far, spreading lies about us, if they stay angry. We might actually find a better welcome in port from here on out with less of his yammer being believed."

"Hopefully. But he'll not stop. You heard him. He means to curtail our 'ridiculous adventures.'" Rafe scowled.

Blackthorne scoffed. "Like he could."

Rafe shrugged. "We'll see, I suppose. Today, it doesn't matter, as we need to be off on one of those adventures. Prepare the ship for sailing, Blackthorne. As soon as the harbour crew is able, we need to be underway for Crickwell Island and Red Bay."

"Aye, Captain. I'll see to it immediately."

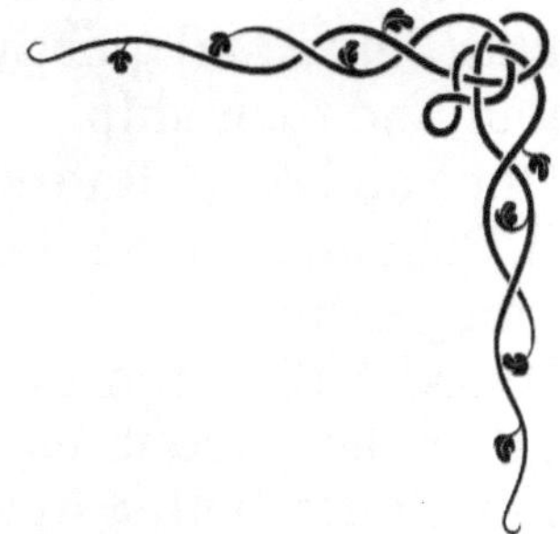

Chapter Five

Red Bay

The quaint harbour town of Red Bay nestled itself in a sheltered cove on the westward side of Crickwell Island. Its only distinction of note was its sheep and the fine wool the animals produced. The *Jewel* sailed into a lively port, the grey harbourside tucked against a picturesque backdrop of bright buildings. Beyond the wharves, quaint homes and shops painted in cheery reds, yellows, blues, and greens greeted them with meadows and pastures stretching beyond the sea.

The ship docked beside the two vessels berthed in the port, noticing sailors loading the town's exports onto the cargo ships. Rafe disembarked with Blackthorne and Short Davy, checked in with the harbourmaster, and then, as a group, walked straight on to the Red Bay Museum and Library.

They found the wooden building just beyond the port, off the west side of the marketplace. It was larger than Rafe expected. Two storeys and painted deep red, trimmed in gold. It had a gilded sign over the doorway, and the men heard the light tinkle of a bell as they entered into a carpeted anteroom bare of furniture. They faced another door leading into the museum proper that was left ajar. The faint smell of perfume drifted and heralded the sound of a feminine voice that beckoned, "Come in, gentlemen. I've been expecting you."

Rafe and his men moved forward, striding into a room lined with bookshelves, cabinets of odd-looking statues, and other artifacts and full of tables with more stacks of books. A petite, raven-haired woman dressed in a long patchwork skirt, a high-collar green blouse, and a dark blue jacket stood in front of a bookcase. Unruly curls of hair sprawled over her shoulders and around her face, the ends tickling the collar of her coat. She smiled at them, an offbeat charm radiating from her expression. She reminded Rafe of a giddy lass with a secret. She walked towards them with a bounce in her step, her heels clicking on the stone tiled floor. When she stopped in front of them, she extended her hand.

"Captain Morrow and crew, I presume."

Rafe nodded, strangely at a loss for words, and shook her hand.

"Wonderful. I'm Miss Theodora Ainslie. Welcome, welcome. Lord Merrill sent word you were coming. It is such an honour and a pleasure to have you visit." She rocked on her toes, and the tone of her voice gushed. "I was informed you were curious about our books and materials on the god, Ashetus? Is that correct?"

"Yes, ma'am." Rafe found his voice and then frowned. He quickly added, "Wait. Did you say, *god*?" He cast her a skeptical look. "Are you certain about that? I doubt this creature has claim to be a god."

"Oh, yes. Definitely a god." She either failed to notice Rafe's skepticism or chose to ignore it, continuing. "Or at least a demigod. All the texts refer to him as some sort of deity, although they don't quite agree on what kind. Some called Ashetus a sea god. Some, a death god or a god of judgement. He's even referred to as the God of Bones. I rather like that one."

"Well now. How interesting. Perhaps a shade of deity, then." Rafe quirked an eyebrow and repressed a snort of disbelief. "Strange though, that I've never heard of him." He paused for a moment to see Miss Ainslie's reaction. She only smiled at him. So he continued. "I must agree with you on the names, though. God of Bones is a most colourful title and perhaps more suitable than sea or death god. My sister and mother aren't known for sharing."

"Your sister and mother..." Miss Ainslie gave a tiny gasp. "Oh my, I forgot. You are rather well-versed in gods, aren't you? My apologies, Captain. I meant no insult on your family tree. I can only go by what's written in the books."

Feeling suddenly contrite at her discomfort, Rafe replied, "No offence taken, ma'am. It's just a bit odd, being lectured on the topic of gods."

She laughed. "I can imagine. I'll try to be less professorial and more mindful of your lineage." She tilted her head and gave him a lopsided grin. "And you didn't just come to listen to me prattle, so if you gentlemen will follow me. We keep all the relevant books in the back room." She turned, crooking her hand, and walked off towards an adjacent room, her curls bouncing against her neck. The three men trailed after her into, yet, another section filled with books.

"I've laid out all the volumes regarding Ashetus, here." She indicated a table with two stacks comprising seven books. "There isn't much, but I can give you a quick overview or answer any questions before you start researching."

"Where did all this information originate, Miss Ainslie?" Rafe tapped the cover of the nearest book with a finger. "Someone must have compiled the stories about Ashetus in these volumes. However, in all my years, I've never heard any mention of this creature.”

“Perhaps it’s because, if I’m not mistaken, you’ve spent most of those years in the Outer Islands. All these books are from the Seven Kingdoms. We’re quite lucky to have received them. Lord Merrill himself donated these copies.”

Rafe quirked an eyebrow. “Did he now? Interesting.”

“Oh, yes. Lord Merrill takes a great interest in the Kingdoms’ and Islands’ history, folklore, and legends. He’s been most generous over the years to Red Bay and many other museums.”

“Really? The man is full of surprises.”

“Oh, indeed. He is quite the scholar and philanthropist, Lord Merrill, and speaks very highly of you, Captain.”

“That’s good to know. Might I ask how he came to acquire these manuscripts and their origin?”

“I have no idea how Lord Merrill manage to acquire the books. The volumes come from the Eastern Kingdom of Idria, which is remarkable as the scholars of that kingdom do not share their works.”

“Well, evidently he’s resourceful, our Lord Merrill.” Rafe smiled. “Does he take a particular interest in this forgotten god? I’m curious to know how he became acquainted with the stories of Ashetus.”

Miss Ainslie smiled back, with a slight blush. “Oh, I doubt Lord Merrill had any interest or inkling of Ashetus prior to your inquiries, Captain. While I believe these books may be the only major references to Ashetus that you will find anywhere, he donated them as part of a ten-volume collection of histories. They are simply lost pieces of the tales we have named *The Time of the World Before the Light*.”

“Now, I’m familiar with that.” Rafe suppressed a grin. “My father shared the history of the realms as bedtime stories when I was a child.”

“Really?” She seemed slightly shocked. “A peculiar choice for a child, I must say. Tales of monsters, horrors, and mayhem." She shook her head with what Rafe assumed to be disapproval.

"My father does have peculiar ways at times. So what do the books contain? I'd like some context."

"Ah, yes. They seem to be translated accounts, based on older writings of a scholar named Osratis who lived several centuries ago in the Idrian city of Antrika. Osratis also wrote later works that became the definitive histories of the Seven Kingdoms."

"Osratis is a name I know. A hermit scholar who was considered to be a prophet. I've heard of his histories as well, but I've never read them." Rafe paused for a moment as a chance memory flickered. "I believe Antrika is also famous for being the home of the Society of the Shadow Guard."

Miss Ainslie grinned. "Oh, indeed. The stories I could tell you. They have a most intriguing history. In fact, there are even rumours that some form of the Society exists today. But that's probably best for another day. You came here to learn of Ashetus." She smiled and continued before Rafe could interject. "The first three books in this collection don't deviate much from the standard Kingdom's history and the more widely known of the texts of Osratis. However, these seven I laid out are a bit of a strange mix. They contain a jumble of the well-known history of the Seven Kingdoms and Outer Islands and previously unseen variations of *The Time of the World Before the Light*. This one," she reached over and plucked a book off the table. "is a complex divergence on the history of the Archipelago of Nightfall from its creation to its banishment beyond the realms. In addition, there is a forty-two page appendix consisting of dire warnings on incurring the wrath of Sea Ghouls."

"I do agree with that. One should never incur the wrath of a Sea Ghoul." Rafe smiled, and Miss Ainslie blushed again.

"I can imagine." She ran her finger along the spine of the book she held.

"Is that where this beast came from?" Blackthorne interjected into the discussion. "From the Archipelago of Nightfall?"

Miss Ainslie turned to the first mate. "Oh, no indeed. In fact, the only passage on Ashetus included in this book refers to how the denizens of the Archipelago feared him and how they welcomed banishment to hide from him even after he was imprisoned."

Rafe inhaled sharply while the other two men turned a shade paler. "The creatures in the Archipelago feared Ashetus? That's what it says?"

"Oh, yes. There's a wonderfully descriptive passage on how they all cowered and trembled. On how their screams of terror shook the mountains and the sky. It makes for a fascinating story..." At the worried looks exchanged between her guests, Miss Ainslie paused in her speech, but then added, "Doesn't it? It's just a story. The Archipelago of Nightfall is a myth...a fable."

"No, ma'am." Short Davy spoke quietly. "It's as real as you or I. We've all sailed there."

"But—but, I never dreamed...I mean I knew some of it wasn't exaggeration or lie, but..." She dropped the book on the table with a *thunk* and sank into a nearby chair.

Rafe knelt down to look the woman in the eyes. "I'd wager most everything in those books of yours is real to some degree, Miss Ainslie, and while I can sympathize with your disbelief, we still need your help. If the creatures that live in the Archipelago were afraid of something, we may all be in a great deal of danger."

She looked at him and squared her shoulders. "Yes, of course." She placed her hand on the discarded book. "This volume has just the one mention of Ashetus in regards to the Archipelago and his imprisonment."

Rafe moved to sit in a nearby chair. "Does it say how

he was imprisoned?"

"No. But this one..." She reached across the table and slid another book out of the pile. "This one speaks of a great battle raging from the sky to the sea between Ashetus, a being called the God of the Hunt, and three great shadow birds. I bookmarked it for you." She flipped the book open to the marked page.

"Yes, here it is." She took a breath and read.

The creatures of the Darkness moaned and shivered, fleeing eternally from the terrible God of Judgement they named Ashetus.

She looked up at Rafe, adding, "This is one of the instances where he is referred to as God of Judgement." Then she continued with her reading.

They cried out for release from their torment, for an end to their ceaseless suffering. For the terrible god pursued them, chasing his prey and granting his victims not only a gruesome death but a dreadful existence beyond death, locked evermore in their bones to serve his needs.

She glanced up for a moment. "It also goes into rather ghastly detail of how he feeds on the dead and that he uses the bones of his enemies as his bed." She shuddered slightly and then continued.

One by one the creatures of the Darkness fell to Ashetus, their screams forever echoing on the winds of the worlds, their bodily remains and souls forever bound to his will.

"Damnation!" Short Davy cursed, his body shuddering. "He sounds like an awful thing."

Miss Ainslie nodded in agreement. "Indeed, but the story does get better. I'll—" A bell chime interrupted her. She replaced the marker in the book and closed it with a smile. "That's the door. If you'll excuse me, gentlemen, let me deal with this new visitor and then we'll continue."

Miss Ainslie walked away towards the front door, leaving Rafe and his men. The group fidgeted in silence for a moment before Short Davy turned to Rafe and exclaimed, "Do you really think this is all true? Is that why we're here, sir?" Fear crept in around the edges of his expression. "Has something dark truly crawled out of the Archipelago or someplace even worse? Is this what we're facing?"

Rafe held back a sigh and answered with the straight truth. "Yes. I believe so."

Davy's face blanched, but, before he could say anything, Miss Ainslie returned.

"Sorry to keep you waiting." She marched back to the table and the stack of books oblivious to the tension in the room. "I forgot about today's delivery of new books, but it's all been taken care of. Shall we resume?" Without waiting for an answer, she picked up the book she had been reading previously and opened it to the marked page. "Ah, here it is. We were just coming to the part about the Hunter." She cleared her throat and resumed her recitation.

Their cries of horror were so loud and far-reaching that they flew past the clouds, beyond the Darkness, to the stars themselves. There, the beseeching pleas were heard by the God of the Hunt and his three companions, the Shadow Birds. It is said the pain of these cries touched the heart of the God of the Hunt. So much so, he grabbed his bow and his horn and leapt from the stars into the Darkness followed by his faithful Shadow Birds. He landed on the earth and not the sea, and shook the ground apart, his impact creating the Outer Islands—

"What? Wait." Rafe held up a hand, interrupting. "Stop reading. This God of the Hunt, he created the Outer Islands?"

"That's what it says. I know most tales say the Outer Islands and the Seven Kingdoms were created when Light came to the World, but—"

"No, that's not it. If this God of the Hunt created the islands, then I know who he is. He's Ulerne, the Hunter. My grandfather." Rafe smiled, ignoring the incredulous look on Miss Ainslie's face. "Continue reading, please."

"Um, as you wish." She turned back to the book.

The God of the Hunt roared, his voice challenging the god Ashetus to come and do battle. But the God of Judgement refused, sending his servants, his great army of bones, in his stead. The God of the Hunt grew angry at this insult and fought Ashetus' army by sounding his horn and destroying them all.

"I wonder..." Rafe mused, and Miss Ainslie paused. The captain did not elaborate, but merely said, "Go on."

With his army of bones obliterated, Ashetus had no choice but to do battle with the God of the Hunt. The Terrible God rose from the sea on a scream and a wave that reached to the sky and that shook the mountains. The God of the Hunt matched his cry as did the shrieks of the Shadow Birds. For three days and three nights the battle raged. The world shook, the seas boiled, and the clouds shattered. Every creature of the Darkness hid from the War of Gods until, at last, a night-kissed arrow shot from the God of the Hunt's bow, ending the great battle and severely wounding Ashetus. But even then, the God of Judgement did not die, but fled to lick is wounds far down in the sea into the depths of the Darkness. Yet, the God of the Hunt did not follow, only plucked a star from his home and imprisoned the Terrible God in eternal sleep. There the God of Judgement lies in slumber where only the shadows will have the power to wake him.

"A star?" Blackthorne's droll tone broke into the silence that followed the reading. "A god plucked a star from the sky to imprison this thing? I doubt we'll be stopping anything by those means, sir."

"Not something easily repeated, I grant you, Blackthorne. Does the book say anything else, Miss Ainslie?"

"Only some passages about the Shadow Birds. How two of them were killed by Ashetus and the third was wounded. Here the story becomes unclear." She flipped a few pages of the book and read.

Mourning the deaths of its brothers, the last Shadow Bird remained alone, cast aside by the God of the Hunt, abandoned to its bitter anger. It wandered the world, a Crow.

She closed the book and looked up to see Rafe and Blackthorne exchange another knowing look.

"Does that have some significance?"

"Perhaps. It is not the first time of late we heard mention of a crow. It wouldn't surprise me if it's involved in this matter."

Miss Ainslie sighed. "You really do live a strange life, Captain."

"I am aware." Rafe grinned. "Now, are there any books that tell of the origin of Ashetus, where he came from?"

She reached over and grabbed yet another book. Several bookmarks peeped out from between its pages. She turned to the first marked place. "This is the only reference."

Ashetus, Weaver of Darkness, Keeper of Sea. Creature of whim and beasts, he ruled serene. Ashetus was content, Ashetus ruled the Darkness, ruled the Sea. Until Death broke him. Until Judgement fell. Until he hungered. Then the Terrible God he became. And Death he served, and Death he fought.

She closed the book. "Rather cryptic, I know."

"A bit, but I'm beginning to think I should have asked for a few more family stories growing up." Rafe sighed, knowing far more about Death than he cared to admit to Miss Ainslie. "What else is in these books?"

"Stories about how he killed, his powers, various other dreadful things. I've marked all relevant passages. Why don't I adjourn to the kitchen and make some tea? Then we can go through the rest of them together."

"Tea sounds wonderful, Miss Ainslie." Rafe smiled,

and their host excused herself. He turned to his two crew members. "Grab a book, gentlemen, and start reading." Blackthorne and Davy sat down, each pulling a book from the stack while the sound of a tea kettle echoed from the kitchen.

Chapter Six

Archipelago of Nightfall

The *Jewel* remained in port at Red Bay and the fall of twilight saw Rafe in his quarters mulling over the day's events. A glass of port sat untouched by an open bottle of wine. Rafe simply stared at the dark red liquid and the fading sunlight flickering through the window reflecting off the glassware. Only a knock at the door broke his reverie.

"Come in."

The door swung open and Blackthorne entered. He settled down in a chair. "You've been brooding down here for hours. Would you like to talk about today?"

"I haven't been brooding. Much. I'm trying to understand what today means in terms of many things, but perhaps it might help to talk." Rafe sighed. "So much of what we learned is familiar, yet...why didn't I know the story of Ashetus?" Rafe shook his head. "So many times growing up I heard the tale of the Creation of the World. How Ulerne the Hunter leapt from the stars to the world below. How, when he arrived, he shook the world apart, forming the Seven Kingdoms and the Outer Islands. My grandfather brought the light of the stars to the world before returning to his home." Rafe stared at Blackthorne, and added, "Most of that is written in those books. Why didn't I know the rest of the story?"

"I can't say, sir, but perhaps your grandfather kept his secrets from everyone."

"Interesting. You're saying perhaps my father didn't know of Ashetus?" Blackthorne nodded. "Possible. But I'm betting my mother did."

"Sir?" Blackthorne shifted uncomfortably in his chair. The captain rarely mentioned his mother.

"Yes. You remember the line from one of the books, 'And Death he served, and Death he fought?'"

"I do."

"That, my friend, may very well be a reference to my mother." Rafe leaned back in his chair ignoring the pained look on Blackthorne's face. "She lived here before my grandfather came. In fact, she and my father shaped the beginning of the world we know today. As the story goes, Ulerne sent his son, Reis, to the mortal world to look after his new creation. Some of the creatures that lived there welcomed their new god and the light of the stars, but some refused. Reis banished them to the Archipelago of Nightfall to live in the darkness, yet always under the light of the Perpetual Moon."

"That story I'm quite familiar with, sir. My granny used to tell me about the Archipelago, and warn me never to go to sea." Blackthorne grinned.

"Yet, here you are. Your granny must not have instilled enough fear in your young soul."

"Until I met you, captain, I thought she was quite mad."

"Families, eh?" Rafe chuckled. "The Archipelago was how my parents met, at least, that's what I was told. My mother, Goddess of Death, joined with father to help exile the creatures that rejected the light. Then, together, they fashioned the Mortal World and the After World. So you see, my mother would have known of Ashetus, yet never a word was spoken of him to the gods. I'm beginning to think much of what I was told as a child is a lie or, at the very least, not the whole truth."

Blackthorne shrugged. "That does put another spin on things. It seems very deliberate. That Ashetus was intentionally erased from your history."

"Perhaps. But not erased entirely from the mortal world. It makes no sense. Why hide him from only the gods?" Rafe shifted in his chair.

Blackthorne suddenly fell silent, staring at his boots.

Rafe waited until he could stand the silence no longer. "What is it, Blackthorne? You've thought of something."

"It's just, well sir, perhaps we mortals didn't matter. If this Ashetus exists, a thing like that...no ordinary person could threaten to free it. From what we've learned, I'm not certain even a magic user could manage it. It took a god and the power of the stars to imprison it. Perhaps..." He hesitated slightly. "Perhaps it was thought best to remove temptation from your family."

Rafe drew in a quick breath, the implications sinking in. "You think a god is responsible for these strange happenings?"

Blackthorne nodded. "It is a distinct possibility. Or the Nightmare Crow. It seems an odd coincidence, your sister invoking that name on the Isle of Bones, and then mention of Shadow Birds and a Crow surfacing in relation to Ashetus."

"It does, and you may be right. This creature, whatever it is, may be repeating the same ploy it tried with the Moon Goddess, turning gods against each other." Rafe abruptly slammed his fist on his desk rattling his wine glass, nearly spilling the port. "If only we—"

"Captain!" A fearful shout from above decks interrupted him, and both he and Blackthorne jumped to their feet. They raced to the main deck in all haste. As they emerged, they saw the crew silent and still, all eyes raised to the sky. Above their heads, floating beside the rigging and batting at a sail, hovered the Goddess of the Moon. She looked down when she spotted Rafe.

"Brother. At last. I was beginning to get bored." She laughed and descended slowly alighting with a skip to the main deck.

"Hello, sister." Rafe uncertain whether to be happy, irritated, or afraid settled on a brief smile. "You do know it is customary to ask permission to board a ship, don't you?"

"Of course. But when have I ever been customary?" She spun about with another laugh. "Hello, brother. Hello, brother's crew. I've come for a visit. Shall we have tea?"

"Perhaps we'll just adjourn to my quarters and talk. Before someone does something they'll regret." He eyed the wary and terrified looks shadowing the faces of his men, Blackthorne's included.

"Don't be silly. We're all friends now. Aren't we, brother's crew?" She laughed, a sound more akin to sending shivers over the skin than reassurance. Murmurs rippled through the ship, and a few men backed away a few steps. She laughed again. "See, all friends."

"Stop playing with them, Manume. Let's talk in my quarters."

"Very well." She walked past him and descended below decks, followed by her brother. Every other man remained on deck.

The pair of gods moved through the suddenly deserted corridors and entered Rafe's quarters. Manume walked over to his desk and perched herself on its edge, staring out the window.

"Such a cage you live in, looking out the glass at a broken world."

"Why are you here, sister? Is something wrong? Are you here to stir up mischief?"

"No, no, I am done. My word still holds. I come for a

visit. For a talk. Nothing more." She turned and smiled at him. "Have I not been a good girl so far?"

"Yes, you have. And thank you for keeping your children in check. The seas have been much quieter, less dangerous."

"I try." She rocked on the edge of the desk. "Sometimes they listen. Sometimes they don't."

"I can imagine. But still, I wonder at the timing of your visit."

She shrugged. "What is time? A little bug on a wheel. Spinning, spinning, round and round. Back to the beginning, back to ground." She turned again to the window. "Hugh thought I should come."

Rafe crossed to his desk, and sat down, surprised by her words. "Really? So how is Hugh?"

"He has planted a garden. With flowers. He is a very strange man."

"A garden? Where did he get flowers on the Isle of Bones?"

She shrugged again. "He has been making friends. They give him gifts. Sometimes, they tell him things." She looked at Rafe once more and smiled. "And sometimes my children tell me things."

A shiver ran through Rafe's blood. "Is that why you're here?"

She nodded.

He did not want to ask, but the words spilled out. "What things?"

"Cold magic under the sea. Disappearing bodies. A hungry thing, very old. They are afraid, my children and Hugh's friends." She looked out the window. "Bad things are coming. Things called by shadows and feathers. I can feel them through the moon. Sad voices. Sad, sad voices. And angry ones. Ones that are afraid." She hopped off the desk and faced her brother. "You need to come. You need to talk to Hugh's friends. They will talk to you, tell you things. I don't know why, but they said they would."

"Go where?"

"The Archipelago of Nightfall, of course. Tonight."

"Tonight? Manume, I just can't sail out of port on a moment's notice. I need—"

"Shush, brother, shush! You spend too much time being not a god. You forget. I don't need a ship, silly. We leave tonight, and I'll return you the next day. Easy and done." She held out her hand. "Like when we were children."

Rafe rose, crossed in front of his desk, and took her hand. "I'll need to tell the crew I'm leaving."

"Done. This will be easier on deck. Less rumble and more sparkle."

Rafe chuckled. "Let's try not to wake the town or frighten anyone."

"You always want to steal the fun." She smiled. "Come then, back to the air and the sky!" She moved to the door and yanked it open, tugging her brother along in her wake, and they both went back on deck. As they emerged, crewmen carefully backed to the rail giving them or, more aptly, her, a wide berth. The Goddess of the Moon laughed. "What? Still no tea?"

Blackthorne moved forward a step. "I'd be happy to brew a nice pot of dark leaf, ma'am, if you're staying."

Manume tilted her head. "I like this one, brother." She moved a few paces towards the first mate. "Alas, alas, not tonight, no, no. Not tonight for tea. But maybe someday, little man. Little Blackthorne." She turned, oblivious to his shocked look and addressed Rafe. "Shall we, brother? The night ticks, ticks, ticks away like a bug on a wheel."

"You're right." He took a breath, his voice booming to his men. "I need to take a small trip with my sister. I'll be back by tomorrow with any luck. Until then Blackthorne has command of the *Jewel*." He reached out and grasped his sister's hand. "The quarterdeck is the best place for this. Come along."

Chased by gasps and whispers and the still shocked stare of Blackthorne, the pair raced to the higher deck, and in one, two, three blinks, a wave of moon magic engulfed them both and they vanished from the ship.

Rafe staggered as they hit the sandy beach on the Isle of Bones. He fell to one knee and took several deep breaths.

"See, see." Manume leaned over him and scolded. "Too hard playing at being not a god. You're out of practice. You never used to be bothered by my magic. You used to help more. You'll need to be more of a god, less of a captain."

Rafe lifted his head, gazing at his sister bathed against the light of her perpetual moon. "You may be right. Travelling with you didn't used to be that draining or disorienting."

"Maybe you're just getting old."

Rafe snorted. "Then what does that make you, *older* sister?"

"Prettier." She grinned. "And smarter."

Rafe chuckled and scrambled to his feet as a voice echoed over the dunes.

"You brought him! Hurrah!"

Rafe turned to see Hugh Corwin racing towards them while Manume shouted back.

"I said I would, silly man. Did you doubt?"

"No, of course not." Hugh skidded to a stop with a grin plastered on his face. "Good to see you again, Captain." He held out his hand and Rafe shook it heartily. "I just wish it were under better circumstances."

"So do I. My sister tells me you have new friends, and they want to talk to me." Rafe inhaled and asked, "Is this about Ashetus?"

Hugh sucked in his breath. "How did you hear that name?"

"A ship went aground on Razor Reef and certain oddities about the wreck led me to some new histories regarding the gods and Ashetus."

"Things may be worse than I thought." Hugh sighed and then asked, "What ship?"

"The *Coral Rose*. Out of Abersythe."

"No!" Hugh flopped down on the sand. "I knew men from that ship, saw her in port, drank with her crew." He raised his head looking at Rafe. "What happened?"

"She was swamped by a rogue wave formed in a calm sea. Forced on to the rocks. And then...then, as told by the lone survivor, bones reached up from the sea and dragged the remaining crew under the surface."

"Oh, oh!" Manume interrupted and danced frantically on the sand. "I know about bones!" Hugh and Rafe stared at her, their conversation discarded. "Old bones, new bones, scared bones, the bones whisper. Yes, they do. Whisper, whisper." She stopped moving and tilted her head. "Save me, save me. Little cries, frightened cries. Save me from the Bone Snatcher. From the Keeper. It's why they came here, still come sometimes. Why they stay. The bones know. Yes, the bones know. Where to go. Where to hide."

"What are you saying, sister?"

She smiled and twirled. "Brother, brother, why do they call it the Isle of Bones? Because they are here. In the dirt, in the sand. But where, oh, where did the little bones come from? The old and dead, the bones that fled. Fled, long, long ago. From a bad, bad thing." She pushed some sand with her foot. "They're still afraid. Of this Ashetus maybe. *Ashetus*." She spat as if the name put a bad taste in her mouth. "Sour name, rotten name. Don't like it. Don't like him."

"That actually makes sense, fits with what I've learned."

"It does?" Hugh cast Rafe a skeptical look.

"Of course it does, silly man. My brother knows things. Found out some secrets, I think." She giggled. "Didn't you, brother?”

“Perhaps. An old friend of yours may be involved. The Nightmare Crow.”

She scowled and spat again. “Not a friend. Bad bird. Nasty bird. Don’t like him either.” She stamped her foot. “You two go. Talk to Hugh’s friends. Good friends. They will tell you more secrets. I will listen to some bones and see what they whisper.”

She made a shooing motion with her hands and then walked away across the dunes and grass. Rafe leaned down and helped Hugh to his feet. “She’s right. Let’s go talk to your new friends shall we?”

Hugh led Rafe southwest along the beach to a small secluded cove. The moonlight reflected off the tranquil sea and silence. Not even the wind blew, and the still air only enhanced the quiet. When Hugh spoke, his voice echoed like a drumbeat of thunder.

“They’ll know we’ve arrived and will show themselves in a moment.” He fidgeted, before adding, “They’re from the Island of Stone and Ruins Key, so be prepared.”

As the last word left his mouth, the sea beyond the cove rolled and heaved and three stone giants rose from the water. Rafe stared at the bipedal creatures made of red and grey rock, feeling something akin to awe and fear. Each possessed two arms and a head, but no visible eyes. That oddity caused a shiver to race up Rafe’s spine. Together, they opened their mouths and clacked the stone teeth within. From the ocean, sprung five flying, hissing serpents who lashed their tails and wings.

“Is he the one?” The voices of the stone giants rumbled, shaking the air around Rafe and Hugh.

“Yes,” the serpents replied. “Can’t you smell the stench of god on him? Of power?” The flying beasts circled the three giants. “Strong. Stronger than any I’ve felt since the first one." The five creatures hissed. "But not all light. No, no. Darkness, sweet. Sweet darkness inside. Interesting." The serpents flew lower, hovering just above the water in a semi-circle around the giants.

"Yes, interesting." The giants' rumbling voices washed across the cove again. "You have done well, Hugh. The flying ones say he will do."

With a great grinding noise, the three giants turned their heads in unison, somehow staring at Rafe, even without eyes. The captain shivered, disconcerted by their attention.

"You are god? Blood of the Hunter? Blood of the one that came from the light in the sky? The one called," the voices of the giants paused and then pronounced the name. "*Ul-erne*?"

"Yes. Ulerne was my grandfather."

"Goooood." The voices rolled the vowels in the word like a wave crashing on shore. "What do you know of his battle with the Terrible One? *Ashe-tus*."

"I know they fought, and Ashetus was defeated." Rafe replied softly, tucking away the fact that the giants had not called Ashetus a god. "I know Ulerne imprisoned him." Rafe took a breath, squaring his shoulders. "And I suspect Ashetus has been set free." Behind him, he heard Hugh's soft curse.

The giants shook and the serpents hissed, whipping their tails. The sea swept upon the beach in wave, and the ground quivered. The giants' voices bellowed, forcing Rafe and Hugh to cover their ears and strive for footing as the earth under their feet shifted and heaved.

"We warned him! Warned him!"

For several minutes the serpents and the giants moaned, the cove echoing in a haunting anguish. Then it quieted and the giants spoke, "He was weak, the Hunter. *Mer-ci-ful*. He would not kill the Terrible One. We warned, we warned. Prison would not hold, not eternally. Kill we said, kill. He could. Only he could, but he did not. Death herself begged him, but he did not kill."

"Mother was there?" The words slipped out to Rafe's immediate regret.

The serpents screeched, flying in a frenzied circle until the giants plucked them from the sky. "Shush, flying ones!"

They released the creatures, and the serpents retreated behind the giants as they addressed Rafe once more. "You are blood of Death?"

Rafe nodded. "I think so. I believe my mother is the one you call Death."

"Flying ones. Could this be true?" The giants turned their heads in a scraping groan.

"Yeeessss," the serpents hissed. "The Darkness we saw could be hers."

The giants turned back toward Rafe. "Interesting. Blood of the light, and blood of the dark. That would give this one power. Power like first god, power to wield weapons."

"Weapons?" Rafe interjected. "What weapons? Weapons to fight Ashetus?"

The giants clacked their teeth and a loud snapping sound echoed in the cove. "Not fight. Kill. Must kill *Ashe-tus*."

Rafe took a breath. "I don't have a problem with that." A calm seemed to settle on the giants and the serpents as he said the words. "As long as there are no repercussions. Gods cannot kill gods without..." Here Rafe paused slightly searching for the right word. "I need to know if there will be consequences."

A rumble came from the giants almost as if they were laughing. "No consequences. *Ashe-tus* no full god. Only half. You can kill. If you are strong enough."

Rafe smiled. "I think I can handle it." He showed bravado, even while he wondered if his words were true. But his answer seemed to satisfy the giants. "Now, do you know where I can find these weapons?"

"No." A great rush of air blew from the giant's mouths. A sigh of sorts. "Hidden away. Shifting secrets given to Shadow Guard. Only their song tells where now. Find the song in your world. Song of the First God."

"Find the song?" Rafe repeated, unsure if he heard correctly.

"Yes. Must go now. We must hide. All should hide until you kill the Terrible One." The giants rumbled, starting to sink.

"Wait, wait! One more question! What type of weapons am I looking for? What can kill Ashetus?"

"The horn and the bow. The horn and the bow." The words echoed over the sand as the stone giants and the flying serpents disappeared beneath the sea.

As they watched the creatures depart, Rafe remarked, "Well, that was fascinating. It's not every day you have a conversation with some of the Old Ones." Then he turned to Hugh. "May I ask how you befriended the Stone Giants *and* the Wind Drakes?"

Hugh shrugged. "When she goes off, I get bored, so I explore. One day I found a boat and repaired it. Then I started travelling to the other islands in the Archipelago. The Stone Giants liked to talk." He shrugged again and kicked at a pebble. "The Wind Drakes, well, they found me when everyone got spooked. The creatures that live here are afraid and want help."

"So why not go to my sister?"

Hugh chuckled. "She confuses them."

Rafe smiled. "Now that I understand."

"Bah." A familiar voice came out of the shadows and the Goddess of the Moon stepped into view. "They don't listen well enough. Don't listen." She walked past them and stared out at the water. "They don't listen." She wheeled around to face Rafe and Hugh. "But I listen. Listened to the bones. Yes, I did. They said many things. About birds, and horns, and mothers who sing. Told me what to do, they did."

Rafe sighed. "What do you know, Manume?"

"Not what I know, but what I did. To send you on your path, little brother. Away, away to kill the bad thing with the bad name. Back to your ship tonight you go, then sail away to your new Oracle and the ghostly girl who killed your favourite. Lynna will meet you on the way. She will tell you about the song. A mother's lullaby."

"Lynna? The song? Manume what do you—"

"Shush. No more talk." She walked up to her brother and grabbed his hand. "Not to me, not me. Sail your ship. Talk to Lynna. Now I take you back. I have other things to do, strange people to see."

Rafe sighed again. "Very well. I'll go back and do as you ask. I'll sail on the tide to see the Oracle."

"Good, good." She tilted her head and looked at Hugh. "Go home, Hugh. I'll be back soon."

In a flash of light and a swirl of magic, the pair of gods vanished, leaving behind the waves, the moonlight, and a solitary ghost shaking his head.

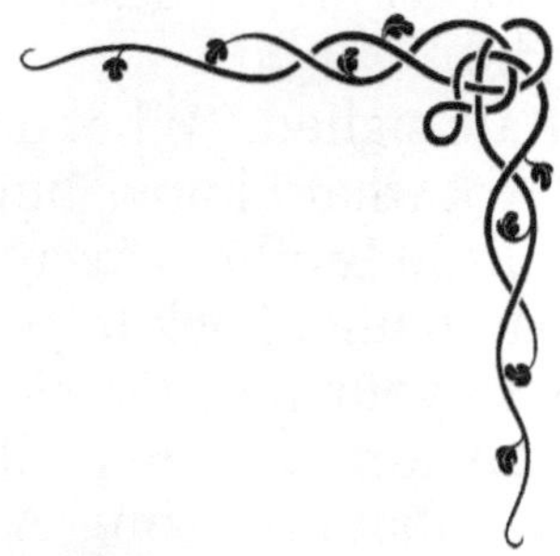

Chapter Seven

Songs of the Sea

"Just once, Blackthorne, I would like one of the beings I come across to speak plainly. To say 'go here' and 'do this.' Is that too much to ask?" Rafe sighed in exasperation. He sat in his quarters across from his first mate, half a day's sail out of the Red Bay harbour. "And they wonder why I prefer mortals. At least you lot don't often speak in riddles."

"Yes, sir. It would be nice. Perhaps, at our next stop, someone will hand you a nice detailed map of where to go with instructions on the back of how to vanquish ancient resurrected gods." Blackthorne smiled and Rafe chuckled.

"Even better, my friend. But for now, we must contend with the fact that we're sailing to Rock Island on the advice of my sister who talks to bones. And somewhere along the way, my other sister will show up to sing me a song that will supposedly lead us to weapons powerful enough to kill this new threat."

"At least we have a confirmation of sorts that this Ashetus exists and he's what we're facing. And we have a plan to defeat him. Even if it is a peculiar one."

"I suppose. We are better off than we were yesterday. I just wish things were simple."

Blackthorne snorted. "Life around you, sir, is many things, but simple is not one of them."

Rafe laughed. "Too true, Blackthorne, too true."

A knock sounded on the door, and Pinky Jasper poked his head in the room without waiting for permission to enter. "Begging your pardon, Captain, there's a waterspout off the starboard side. Behaving strangely. Could be...um... your sister arriving."

Rafe glanced at Blackthorne who shrugged. "Well then, shall we go see what's next in this mess?" The captain and the first mate rose and followed Pinky above deck. One glance showed him his sister had indeed arrived and Rafe barked an order as his foot hit the boards.

"Match speed with the waterspout, Mr. Anders, and the rest of you lot make way for our guest!" He walked to the rail and shouted, "Come aboard, Lynna!"

In answer, the spout abruptly veered towards the ship and burst apart in a spray of water, drenching both the *Jewel* and its crew in an unexpected shower of seawater. A lithe, naked woman gracefully tumbled through the air and the raining ocean to land safely on deck beside Rafe.

Lynna glowered at him. "Let's get this over with. Privately."

"In my quarters, perhaps? Below deck?"

"Fine." She marched past him, ignoring the stares and averted glances of the crew, and climbed below deck. Rafe hurried after her, shaking water from his coat and hair. He caught up to his angry sister and escorted her to his cabin. He sat down at his desk while Lynna, trailing water across the floor, paced like a caged animal.

"What is going on?" She yelled, seemingly at the wall. Rafe waited, letting her rant. "Do you know what's happening under the sea? It's chaos. Every creature, every one, is terrified. All I hear is, 'bones, bones, the bones are coming,' or 'the Terrible One. Save us. Save us!' They're all trying to hide. To flee." She whirled, glaring at her brother. "And the sea doesn't feel right anymore. It's different. It's darker. I can't explain it. It's like something else is reaching out, trying to take control." Lynna shivered. "And that's not the strangest thing. Those who have drowned, their corpses have disappeared from their resting places. There's an underwater reef where the bones of an old sailor rested. They're gone, disappeared. Every scrap of his remains vanished one day. What's going on?"

Rafe sighed, Lynna's words confirming his worst fears and banishing any hope he was chasing a fool's errand.

"There have been rumblings from the After World as well. Souls in pain, souls gone missing. I think something old and powerful has awakened, something from before the gods."

"From before the… is that why Manume was babbling about bones and your mother's lullaby?" Lynna stopped pacing. "She insisted I tell you."

"My mother's lullaby?"

"Yes, something she sang to you when you were a baby. I used to sneak in and listen. It never made sense, but I loved her voice. I tried singing it once or twice to Manume when we were young, but she never wanted to listen. Until now."

"Didn't make sense how?" Rafe leaned forward, all his attention on his sister.

"The lyrics seemed dark for a lullaby, and I'm sure, what she sang was only part of the song. But it was strangely compelling, and I've never forgotten it." She inhaled a breath and stared at her brother. "I never forgot, almost like I couldn't forget."

A prickle ran along Rafe's skin. "What were the words, Lynna? I need to hear the song. It could be the key to stopping this threat."

"A song?" Lynna's voice dropped incredulity like

the clouds dropped rain. Her demeanour changed from troubled to amused.

Rafe suppressed a smile. "Yes. A song."

"If you insist." Lynna closed her eyes and sang, her voice clear and sweet and soothing as a summer sea.

Hush, hush, close your eyes,
Against the night.
Hush, hush, the stars will shine,
Against the night.

The horn will sound.
The bones will fall.
The Hunter stalks the Terror.

Against the night,
The bow will sing.
The beast will die,
Underneath the raven wing.

So, listen well, oh, brave new soul,
And stand against the night.
Find the horn, and find the bow,
Along the Path of Sorrows.

Lynna fell silent, and Rafe sighed. "That's it?"

She nodded. "As I said, I think there's more, but she never said. You could always go ask her."

Rafe gave her a sour look. "That would take too long. The last time I went to her Underworld, it took six months. And she still refused to see me."

"Oh. I didn't know." Lynna looked away with a sigh. "I've never tried to visit her after she left." She sighed again. "Neither of us had much luck with mothers, did we? Ours turned their backs on their children, left us." She turned to look at Rafe, deep sorrow on her face. "Is it a wonder we're the way we are? Prickly outcasts from the gods. It's why I prefer the sea to family."

"And yet, here we are, pulled into the middle of a family mess." Rafe nodded at Lynna's surprised look. "Oh, yes, this is a family legacy. Whatever is happening, it seems to be grandfather's doing."

"That far back? Father told stories, but..." She let the words hang, and Rafe understood. Their father always kept his secrets.

Rafe nodded. "I know. Which is why I'm grasping at straws and old songs. Can you think of anything else? Do you have any idea what the 'Path of Sorrows' is?"

"No," She hesitated, then added, "But your temple at Rock Island might. It's something, something odd. Your Oracle comes to mind when I hear that phrase." She reached out as if to touch her brother then let her hand fall. "I'm sorry. I can't help more. Is there anything else I can do?"

"Just stay safe and listen. I may need your help in this. I may need a lot of help."

"You have my support, brother." This time she did extend her hand, and he shook it. They walked back to the deck where they said goodbye before Lynna returned to her ocean.

The sun stretched close to midday at the hour that the *Jewel* sailed into Blue Bay. After a quick report to the harbourmaster, Rafe and Blackthorne headed to the Temple.

"So, your sister wasn't much help, then?"

"She confirmed my mother's involvement and gave me part of the song, for all the good that did. Apparently, the bow and the horn we seek are on the 'Path of Sorrows.'" Rafe shook his head. "Why the cryptic reference? Why not say it directly? Like they're in the Fire Islands or locked away on Tenby Key. These riddles and clues are ridiculous."

Blackthorne shrugged, and Rafe lapsed into silence until they reached the temple. There they rang the bell and gained entry. High Priestess Rayla met them in the main hall.

"Welcome, God of Souls." She smiled at Rafe and then at his first mate. "And you as well, Mr. Blackthorne. Have you come about the disturbance the Oracle has sensed?"

"I would think it probable as there is some dark threat looming. What has the Oracle seen?"

"She should tell you that herself. She is in her chambers with that—that ghost you left us."

"Captain Erikson?" Rafe frowned, a bit of revulsion stirring in his blood. "What is she doing with the Oracle?"

"I do not understand it, but the child has taken pity on her or something. The Oracle says she is important." Rayla scowled. "I do not like it, but I must accept it."

Rafe inhaled then let out the breath slowly. His sister's face danced against moonlight in his memory.

"The ghostly girl who killed your favourite." The whisper slipped into the air and swirled against the tension.

"What did you say?" Rayla snapped the question and then looked contrite. "My apologies, Exalted One. I did not mean to be so cross."

"No need, I understand. I meant no offence. It was just something my sister said. I think the Oracle is right. Like it or not, Erikson may be important."

Rayla scowled. "I do not like it, but I will tolerate it. Come with me." With a sigh, Rayla led the pair in to see the Oracle.

They heard laughter as they entered, and a smiling fifteen-year-old girl glanced up at them, locks of her red hair falling over her face. Beside her, the ghost of Captain Eva Erikson giggled until she saw Rafe.

"Why is he here, Jainna?" Erikson tried to cower

behind the Oracle's chair.

"Not for you, dear." The girl replied in a soothing tone. "Not directly, at any rate." She smiled again. "Come and sit, God of Souls, and ask your questions."

Rafe crossed the room while Rayla and Blackthorne remained by the door. He sat in a chair nearest the Oracle while Erikson whimpered.

"Shush, dear. Shush." The Oracle spoke soothingly, directing her remarks to Erikson. "No one's going to hurt you." A snort of derision came from the direction of Rayla, but everyone ignored it. "Speak your questions." The Oracle repeated her words, turning her attention back to Rafe. "We'll give you what answers we can."

With a touch of disquiet, Rafe asked, "What do you know of a being called Ashetus, of the bow and horn of Ulerne the Hunter, and something called the Path of Sorrows?"

The young Oracle sat back in her chair, an enigmatic smile lingering on her lips. "Of Ashetus, very little. I've heard the name whispered in my dreams these past weeks and have seen his red eyes haunting me in my visions. But that is all." She placed her hands neatly in her lap, her fingers smoothing the folds of her dress. "Of Ulerne and his weapons, I know of an old tale murmured in my ear as I slept. A tale of how he concealed his weapons, placed them in the care of a trusted few. That is all I can say of Ulerne." She paused, drumming her fingers on the arm of her chair. "But the question of the Path of Sorrows that is easily answered. That is the name of a song." She giggled. "An odd little thing. My mother used bits and bobs as warnings for her children. 'Ward against the night,' she'd say or 'don't chase the Path of Sorrows.' It's quite a popular ditty on Tenby Key."

"Then that's where I will need to look next, I suppose."

"No." A frightened whisper crept out of Erikson's mouth. Rafe looked at her quizzically. "If you want the whole song, every bit, see Old Mother Abel on Outcast Key." Erikson glanced at the Oracle and then at Rafe before continuing. "The strains sung on the islands aren't what you're looking for. They're only watered down, rewritten pieces. But Old Mother Abel, she'll have the original. Pristine and perfect. She collects things, you see, for certain people. Keeps them tucked away, and I know she has that song written down." Erikson paused, but finished with, "She told me once, a long while back. Bragged about it. Laughed really."

"I see." Rafe glared. "You did business with Old Mother Abel. Why am I not surprised?"

Erikson bristled. "Well it's a good thing I did, now isn't it? You be needing what she has and all? And that's not..." Erikson abruptly frowned. "That's not all. No, I remember now. She said I would relay the message one day for the Shadow Guard. I thought it odd at the time." She stared at Rafe. "But that's what I'm doing, isn't it?"

"Yes, I suppose it is." Rafe sighed, the sound a mixture of confusion and irritation at yet another mention of the strange Society of the Shadow Guard. "And you may not be the only one." He glanced at young Jainna.

"You have much work ahead, God of Souls." The Oracle broke into the space between the pair before Rafe could pursue his errant thoughts. "And we can be of no more help. Whatever rises will not be found by me. You will need others to guide you in this journey. Go where we pointed you and find your way."

Rafe nodded, letting his further questions go. "Thank you, Oracle. The aid offered is enough." He rose and took a step to leave, but then turned back unexpectedly struck by something she said. "One more question. Who whispered to you in your sleep?"

The girl stared, her dark green eyes reminding him of seaweed in the sunlight.

"Death whispered to me. Death."

Rafe sighed. "Of course she did." He nodded to the

young girl. "Thank you, Oracle. Thank you."

Then he and Blackthorne took their leave and returned to the ship.

Chapter Eight

Attacks

"Go see Old Mother Abel? You're not seriously considering this? Are you mad?" Blackthorne's shout shook the beams in the captain's quarters. "Respectfully, sir," he added on seeing Rafe's amused look.

"I know. I have no wish to visit the old crook any more than you, but she is the one who has a copy of this blasted song."

"Are we sure of that? We only have the word of Erikson. Can we trust her after what she did? After what you did to her?"

"If you had asked that yesterday, I would have said we cannot. But you saw her. She volunteered the information. I believe what Erikson said to be true." Rafe studied a small spot on his desk not looking Blackthorne in the eye. "So does the Moon Goddess."

"Now we're desperate enough to listen to the word of all our old enemies, are we?"

Rafe looked up, hearing the cross tone in Blackthorne's

voice, and snapped, "I suppose we are."

Blackthorne sighed and flopped in a chair, his argument nearly spent. "But Mother Abel? You know that old crone will want something in return for her help. She's a deceitful old thief and liar, and she can't be trusted."

"I know, but we won't be arriving at Outcast Key for a few days, I've sure we can devise a way to appease the woman by then." Rafe smiled, trying to put a brighter spin on their problems. "In the meantime let's enjoy the day on deck. We're in full sail, with a good wind and a warm sun." He rose from his chair, coaxing Blackthorne to do the same. They walked up the main deck, the hum of the ship surrounding them.

"See, a beautiful day." Rafe clapped Blackthorne on the shoulder. "Let's go appreciate it on the quarterdeck."

Rafe persuaded a still gloomy Blackthorne to the upper deck and they stood at the rail staring at the blue sky and the bouncing waves.

"Cheer up," Rafe nudged his first mate. "Look out at the sea. A perfect day for sailing."

"It is that. On days like these, it is easy to forget your troubles." The frown on Blackthorne's face eased.

Rafe smiled. "That's the spirit—"

"Captain! Something's in the water! Starboard side!"

Rafe snatched up a spyglass as Blackthorne's voice chimed, "You were saying...about it being a perfect day?"

Rafe ignored the gibe and scanned the water. He spotted the disturbed patch, a place where the sea churned and figures writhed under the surface keeping pace with the ship. Definitely not bones or corpses. No, these were familiar shapes. He reached out with his magic...

"Hard to port! Hard to port!" The captain shouted the order as the sea to starboard exploded in a spray of water and angry shrieks. Rafe heard the cry of 'Sea Ghouls!' from his crew as the ship lurched, executing the hard turn. Three creatures shot into the sky flying over the ship, their screeching voices vibrating the masts. One dove down, shredding a topsail while the others sliced through some rigging. Sailors scrambled from their perches ducking claws and gnashing teeth as the ghouls wailed their way around the ship. Quiet Peter raced to his post and rang the ship's bell, loud and long. For a tiny fraction of a moment, the ghouls screamed, backing away before rushing to the attack once more.

Rafe raced to the starboard rail, his heart pounding, the ineffective peals of the bell ringing in his ears. Something was wrong. He could feel another presence, a force in control of the ghouls, blocking his influence and counteracting his power.

A force exerting authority over creatures only he should be able to command.

Anger welled in his mind, a fire burning through his blood. And behind the anger, fear. If something else commanded the ghouls...Rafe shivered. Still, he had to try to turn them back before they tore apart the ship.

"Stop! How dare you attack me!" His voice boomed outward on a wave of his energy, cracking the air, slamming into the frantic, circling ghouls. The creatures slowed, hesitating, falling silent. Rafe could feel his power pulling at them. "Retreat! Back to the sea!"

For half a breath Rafe thought he'd won, but something violently pushed back. Dark power ripped through Rafe's tenuous connection to the ghouls and snapped the slim tether of magic. The creatures screamed in fury and the trio dived at the captain. He watched them lunge and, in a mad impulse, he leapt from the ship to meet them, spinning upward on a burst of blue-tinted magic.

Rafe crashed into the three ghouls, shattering their descent with a battering ram of his energy and sending them all flying from the ship. They tumbled through the air, and, when he righted himself, Rafe hovered over the sea surrounded by enraged ghouls. He didn't hesitate, simply summoned his power, and attacked. He showed no mercy.

A wave of magic blasted into the ghouls and they screamed, Rafe's power ripping apart their essence as easily as tearing paper. All three shattered in a thousand echoes of pain, their pitiful broken souls obliterated from any remnant existence in the worlds. The horror of their ending splintered through Rafe, through blood and bone, and he bellowed his grim rage, his voice melding with the death cry of the ghouls. The echo of his magic reverberated across the world, and Rafe felt the intruding darkness reel from the backlash. He relished in the satisfaction of hurting it, this interloper. For a moment he hung there, hovering in the sky, breath heaving, fighting the urge to chase the beast that dared usurp his domain. He looked down at his ship and slowly let some of the anger wash away with the sway of the sea.

Gradually he descended, landing deftly on the quarterdeck beside Blackthorne. "It commanded them." The terse words came out as a growl, and Blackthorne involuntarily moved back a step. "This Ashetus, this *thing*, took control of my Ghouls! My souls! Made me destroy them! I will not have it! I will not tolerate this affront!" Blue sparks snapped from Rafe's fingertips and cobalt fire danced in his eyes. "I will hunt this creature down and end it!"

"I'm all for that, sir," Blackthorne softly spoke while taking another step back. "But we have a bit more pressing problem."

"What could be more pressing than the end of this threat?" Rafe turned to his first mate, his eyes still flashing blue fire. The captain's fingers curled into fists, and Blackthorn took one more step backward hitting the edge of the stair rail.

"The ship, sir. She took damage from the ghouls. They slashed up her sails and rigging. It's a mess, sir. We can limp along for a while, but we should go into port before Outcast Key."

Rafe stood still for several heartbeats, his magic still racing across his skin. He could feel the crew's tension, see the traces of fear in their eyes. He took a breath, and then another, and let his power fade bit by bit. Only then did he speak.

"Head north to Tenby Key. We'll anchor in Riverford and make repairs. Then straight to Outcast Key." He walked away and began moving down the steps to the main deck, pausing halfway. He turned back to look at Blackthorne. "And don't worry anymore about Old Mother Abel. After this, she'll tell us what we want to know or rue the day she was born. I am in no mood for bargaining." He marched down the steps, across the ship, and disappeared below decks to his quarters.

Rafe brooded in his quarters feeling the rock of the docked ship while listening to the shouts and sounds of repair echo from above. Fury still simmered, and it took all his control not to manifest an outward display of his magic. His blood sang with his power, and he could feel the fire in his bones calling for retribution.

At the knock on his door, he wanted to scream, but snapped, "Come in."

Blackthorne walked in the room, keeping his distance, and the door opened. "We may have trouble, sir. Three Navy of the Royal Court ships have sailed into port. They seem to be blockading the harbour entrance."

"What?" Rafe jumped to his feet. "Damnation! What are those fools up to, impeding the right of sail?" He snatched up a spyglass, marched around his desk, brushing past Blackthorne. Rafe raced up to the quarterdeck and trained the spyglass on the navy ships.

"What do they think they're doing? They've sealed

off the harbour entrance and are ferrying men in by jolly boat? That makes no sense." Rafe continued to stare. "Damnation, they're heading our way!" He lowered the spyglass and spat over the rail. "Pelham's put them up to something, I know it. Curse that man."

Rafe leaned against the rail and watched the small boat move ever closer. Around him, the crew continued to work and affect repairs, unsure of what was unfolding. Rafe tracked the navy sailors as they rowed alongside the Jewel, and tied off next to her berth.

"Ahoy, the *Celestial Jewel* and Captain Morrow! Show yourself in the name of the Navy of the Royal Court!"

With a snarl, Rafe bounded down to the main deck and leaned over the gunwale, shouting down to the six sailors bobbing on the water alongside the *Jewel*. "By whose authority do you address this ship and block the harbour entrance? You have no jurisdiction over me or mine!"

"The Navy of the Royal Court has authority to enforce the peace over all the Outer Islands, sir!" The sailor's shouting voice wavered as he addressed Rafe, but he continued. "What's more, we act on the mandate of Commander Augustus Quartermain Pelham, commanding officer of the King's Rock Fort. He has charged that one Captain Rafe Morrow and his crew of the ship known as the *Celestial Jewel* have wantonly broken the accords and regulations of the sea and circumvented the lawful rights of the Navy of the Royal Court!" The sailor plucked a document from his coat and waved it in the air. "We hold a warrant of arrest for Captain Rafe Morrow and the seizure of the *Celestial Jewel* by the sanction of said Navy of the Royal Court!"

"Are you serious?" Rafe yelled his displeasure and disbelief and grabbed the gunwale with both hands. His body sizzled in blue-hued energy and, in one crazed moment, he meant to sink the navy sailors to the bottom of the harbour. Then a voice broke through the madness.

"Don't do it, sir. They're just following orders. Save it for the bastard who deserves it. Pelham."

Rafe stared at the sailors now scrambling for the oars in a fearful attempt to escape and suppressed his rage with a force of will. His sparkling display of magic faded, and he shouted to the panicky sailors.

"Come aboard and serve your warrant. You have safe passage." He turned away with a grunt, whispering under his breath, "For now."

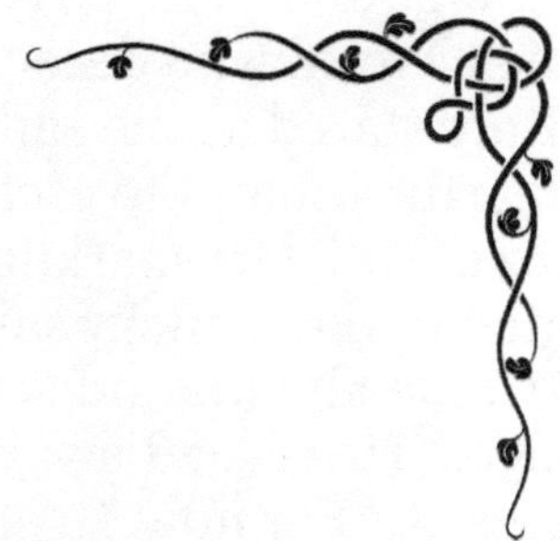

Chapter Nine

Arrest

Five Navy of the Royal Court sailors boarded the *Jewel*. One remained with their boat. Rafe met them at the top of the gangplank, Blackthorne at his heels. The young men clustered close together, darting worried glances at the scowling crew, their hands fingering the hilts of their swords. Their ranking officer, a dark-haired lieutenant, stepped forward, extending a folded document with a trembling hand.

"The arrest and seizure warrant, sir. We have orders to escort you and your ship back to Black Shoals to answer for the charges."

Rafe took the paper and unfolded it. He scanned the contents and the usual Navy of the Royal Court jargon, reading aloud the official charges.

Captain Rafe Morrow, and the crew of the ship Celestial Jewel, are hereby accused of engaging in the unlawful commandeering and interference of Royal Naval duties as laid out by the Seven Kingdoms charter. Furthermore, Captain Morrow is charged with the improper command of an uncatalogued vessel, and the illicit business of transporting unsanctioned cargo.

He folded the paper and handed it back to the sailor. "So, he's finally done it. Overstepped his authority." Rafe smiled and watched the young naval officer shiver. "I'm curious, sailor, what if I refuse to recognize the warrant? How do you plan to enforce it?"

"Sir. I would very much prefer if you would come peacefully. Let our three navy ships escort yours with no trouble. But the fleet's been on the lookout for you and every ship has orders to take you in by force, if necessary."

"Pelham's orders, I take it?"

The officer nodded.

"He really has gone too far this time. Using naval resources for his own vendetta." At Rafe's dark look, the naval officer stepped back, bumping into his fellows.

"Please don't make trouble, sir."

Rafe relaxed his anger slightly. "I won't lieutenant, but you'd best pray trouble doesn't find you anyway, while I'm off dealing with Pelham's mischief. He'll pay for this one way or the other."

"Is that a threat, sir?"

"No, sailor. A promise. Your commander is a fool, and now his arrogant power play has put the Outer Islands in greater danger. This delay in our search may very well get people killed."

The lieutenant looked pained. "I cannot answer to that. Only my own duty. Will you comply with the warrant?"

Rafe sighed. "Yes, lieutenant." As much as he wanted to punch someone, he couldn't fault the sailor for discharging Pelham's repugnant orders. "I'll comply." His crew's gasps and growls contrasted the look of relief on the lieutenant's face. "What's the next step in my arrest?"

"I, and one of my men, stay aboard. The rest of my men return to our navy ship with word of your submission.

Then you allow the three waiting ships to escort you to Black Shoals and the King's Rock Fort to stand trial. Word has been sent by spellcaster to Commander Pelham that we were initiating the arrest. He will have things prepared when we arrive."

"I'm sure he will. Very well, lieutenant. Carry out your duty."

"Thank you, sir." The young man straightened his posture to stand tall and declared in full voice, "Under orders from the Navy of the Royal Court, I, Lieutenant Hughes declare this ship, the *Celestial Jewel*, seized, and its captain and crew under arrest."

Suddenly the deck rumbled, and the ship violently rocked in its berth. Rafe laid a hand on the gunwale and whispered, "Easy, girl. Everything will be all right. Don't fight." He nodded at the lieutenant, the man still ramrod straight despite the fear written on his drawn, pale-as-sea-foam face. "Continue."

Hughes swallowed and turned to the other Navy sailors. "Rollins, you will remain here with me. The rest of you return to the ships and inform them that Captain Morrow will go quietly. As soon as we sail out of port they can unblock the harbour and fall into formation for escort to Black Shoals." He turned back to Rafe. "Is that acceptable, Captain?"

"It is, though we'll need to finish repairs before we sail anywhere. Blackthorne. How long?"

"Half the hour, sir."

"Good. Will that be satisfactory, Lieutenant?"

He nodded and addressed his men. "Inform the ship we will depart upon completion of repairs." He nodded and barked, "Dismissed!" The four men saluted and hurried down the gangplank, back to their jolly boat.

Rafe watched their hasty departure without amusement. He turned to his first mate. "See to the repairs, Blackthorne, and take the ship out of port. You have command until Black Shoals. I have no stomach for this farce." He sighed. "Unless the Navy gives you trouble, I'll keep to my quarters for the trip under the watch of these two." He flicked a hand at the navy sailors. "Come along, Lieutenant Hughes, and...Rollins, is it?" The frightened midshipman vigorously nodded. "You can stand guard outside my quarters for the duration of this trip."

Rafe emerged from his quarters at Black Shoals harbour, his bad mood and anger more under control. His guards trailed him like meek puppies as they disembarked in silence from the *Jewel*. To Rafe's surprise, Lord Merrill was waiting on the dock when he was escorted off the ship.

"Milord, what are you doing here?" Rafe tossed out the question as he and his guards walked past. The nobleman scowled at his escort but fell in step with their march to the fort.

"Shameful business, Captain. Shameful. I'm sorry if I played any part in provoking this disgraceful Pelham."

"No need to apologize, milord. It would have come to a head with or without you."

"Still, I offer my support and have taken the liberty of bringing in a witness to help refute these scurrilous charges. From the Abersythe Harbourmaster Guild."

"Did you? How kind. I have my own proof in that regard." He patted his coat's breast pocket.

"Excellent! I can help as well, as I am privy to your agreement with the Seven Kingdoms."

Rafe smiled. "Then I think the two of us shall put Pelham in his well-deserved place."

Commodore Morris Brayburn, naval magistrate, sat in the makeshift trial room of the King's Rock Fort across the table from Pelham who smiled in smug contentment.

"This had better be worth my time and all this secrecy, Commander. I am not used to having trials for unknown accused and last-minute arrangements."

"You'll see the reasons, sir, when he arrives. He is a dangerous man. I needed to apprehend him and put him on trial with all haste to protect our citizens."

"Still, this is most irregular—" The Commodore was interrupted by a knock and the opening of the far door. He frowned as Rafe entered the room under the escort of two midshipmen and Lord Merrill. "Lord Merrill. Captain Morrow. What are you doing here?"

Rafe smiled. "Weren't you informed, sir? I'm the accused."

"You're the..." Commodore Brayburn turned on Pelham in a fury. "What is the meaning of this, Commander? You've brought the God of Souls to trial? Are you mad?"

"I—I—sir. I mean..." Flustered by the commodore's reaction, Pelham fumbled his words, the smug look on his face dissolving in sudden fear. But his uncertainty lasted only a moment. "What has that to do with it, sir, respectfully? No matter who he is or claims to be, he is not above the law." He turned to Rafe as the captain and Lord Merrill were escorted to the table and took a seat. With the smug look firmly back in place, Pelham added, "I charge his actions are of a criminal nature. They must be curtailed."

"Ridiculous!" Lord Merrill's voice boomed out, cutting off any reply from Rafe or Commodore Brayburn. "These trumped-up accusations are fraudulent and the ploy of a man with a personal grudge against Captain Morrow. Commander Pelham is a disgrace to the Navy of the Royal Court uniform!"

"Lord Merrill? You're involved in this matter as well?" Commodore Brayburn cast a dark glare at Pelham.

"Yes, sir. I engaged Captain Morrow to look into matters concerning the recent wreck of the *Coral Rose*, an action that may have precipitated this show of injustice. I could not, in good conscience, fail to support him today at this unwarranted trial."

"I appreciate your candour, Lord Merrill, and events may bear the truth in your words, but I will be the one to decide if the trial is unwarranted." Commodore Brayburn turned to Rafe. "Have you been served with the charges?"

"I have, and, if you allow me, Commodore, I can clear up the legalities of those accusations in a few moments."

Pelham snorted. "Impossible, I—"

"Be quiet, Commander!" Brayburn snapped. "Captain Morrow has the floor."

"I'll start with the charges of 'the improper command of an uncatalogued vessel and the illicit business of transporting unsanctioned cargo'. I'm assuming both charges stem from your lack of finding a copy of my papers in the Navy of the Royal Court records of operating ships?"

Pelham nodded. "You can't squirm your way out of this one. There are no records cataloguing and authorizing your ship as a legal vessel. There's not even a record of it at a shipyard."

"You are correct. There are no records of the *Jewel*." Rafe smiled. "In the Navy archives, at least." He reached into his coat pocket and withdrew a document. He unfolded it and handed it to the Commodore. "As you can see this is the original charter and authorization for the *Celestial Jewel* as a lawful vessel, sanctioned to ply trade in the Outer Islands."

"Impossible!" Pelham went red in the face. "It's a forgery! There's no such record!"

"Incorrect. If you will note the date, you will see it states the *Jewel* was registered with the Sea Guild out of Abersythe four centuries ago and given its charter. A charter to last in perpetuity."

"Ridiculous!" Pelham gave a snort. "You expect the court to believe that nonsense. I've never even heard of this Sea Guild."

"The Sea Guild was an independent ship and traders guild and one of the founding members of what is now the Outer Islands Harbourmaster Guild, Commander." Commodore Brayburn rolled his eyes. "Learn some history."

Pelham pouted. "That's still doesn't mean he's telling the truth."

Lord Merrill piped up, "We have a clerk from Abersythe in the hall, Commodore, to verify that there is indeed a copy of the *Jewel's* charter on file with the Harbourmaster's Guild as part of the old Sea Guild's records." He chuckled at Pelham's astonished look. "And he's a mite miffed. He's of the opinion the Navy of the Royal Court has contravened its designated mandate and impugned his office."

"He may be right, but his presence won't be necessary. I accept this document as authentic." The Commodore handed the charter back to Rafe who tucked it in his pocket.

"What! How—how—that's—"

"Shut your mouth, Commander." The commodore glared. "The charges of improper command of an uncatalogued vessel have been laid to rest and answered to my satisfaction. They hold no merit and are dismissed." He turned his attention back to Rafe. "Can you answer the remaining charge, of..." He glanced down at the papers in front of him. "'The unlawful commandeering and interference of Royal Naval duties as laid out by the Seven Kingdoms charter.' What? You can't be serious? For Captain Morrow?" The Commodore wore a look of amazement. "Commander Pelham! This is a nonsensical charge!"

"Why? His continued interference in matters of threats and protection is an intolerable affront to the Navy of the Royal Court."

The commodore groaned. "You are a fool, Pelham. Should I inform him, Captain, or would you like the pleasure?"

"You are aware of my charter, then?"

"I am. As is Lord Merrill, I believe. Everyone at this table seems to be aware, with the exception of the commander."

"Then please, educate him." Rafe smiled as Pelham's arrogance crumbled to alarm, and the Commodore's voice boomed across the table.

"Commander Pelham. The charge of unlawful commandeering and interference of Royal Naval duties cannot be laid against Captain Morrow or any of his crew as they are exempt from heeding the authority of the Navy of the Royal Court charter. In fact, they have their own charter granted by the Seven Kingdoms that supersedes the Navy of the Royal Court jurisdiction in matters pertaining to magical or otherworldly threats. In addition, they have the right to investigate any incidents where suspicion of magic is involved." The commodore paused, letting the weight of his words wash over Pelham. "Do you have any evidence that the captain has violated those boundaries as I have laid out?"

Pelham ground his teeth and spit out, "No."

"Then I dismiss the second charge. You are free to go, Captain Morrow, with my apologies."

Lord Merrill let out an undignified whoop and clapped Rafe on the back. As the pair rose to leave, Pelham hissed, "This isn't over, *Captain*."

"Oh, but it is!" Commodore Brayburn slammed his hand on the table with a bang. "You misused naval resources and wasted my time! We are going to have a *very* long chat over your reprehensible conduct, *Commander*!"

Pelham's stricken face gave Rafe a taste of haughty glee as he and Lord Merrill departed.

Chapter Ten

Lull

"So, what exactly do you want from me, Lord Merrill?" Rafe smiled at his guest over a glass of port. After the trial, the captain agreed to ferry Lord Merrill back to Abersythe on the way to Outcast Key, and the pair had withdrawn to his quarters for a long overdue talk. "I gathered from my visit to Red Bay that you know something about this looming threat? Are you keeping secrets?"

"No. I'll admit I was mildly acquainted with the old myths, having briefly studied the books I donated, but never gave them credence until recently...not until odd stories began floating around Abersythe from sailors and fishermen. And, I admit, I was practicing a bit of a deception when I hired you with an ulterior motive to discuss the issue. The *Coral Rose* only brought matters to a head." Merrill sipped his port. "I'm on your side, Captain. Originally, I thought prudence would be the best course in my dealings with you as your reputation can be mercurial. My apologies if it seemed otherwise."

"You knew something was wrong before you hired me?"

"Not knew. Suspected. Had I any proof, I would not have been so circumspect. Until the *Coral Rose*, I only had rumours and tall tales, which could have easily been false."

Rafe nodded, satisfied with Merrill's answers, if somewhat suspicious the man still harboured secrets. "What of Pelham? You seemed to be well informed on his actions."

"I am, but again, that had nothing to do with you until recently. Pelham has the patronage of a fellow nobleman, Lord Varson. Varson, a retired member of the Seven Kingdoms Navy elite, advocates stricter control of the Outer Islands by the Navy of the Royal Court. I am not in favour of that plan. Bad for business. As such, I keep a discreet eye on our arrogant commander."

"Ah. After today, I may have to keep a closer watch on him myself. No doubt he'll be gunning for me again after he licks his wounds. He doesn't seem the type to give up."

"No. Our Commander Pelham hasn't the sense to retreat and I fear he may see you as the biggest obstacle to increase the Navy of the Royal Court's influence here in the Islands. But enough of him. I believe more pressing things are at hand." Lord Merrill held out his empty glass, and Rafe refilled it with more port. "What of this new threat? Does this Ashetus creature truly exist? Miss Ainslie was kind enough to fill me in on your visit to Red Bay."

"I believe so. And his power is growing stronger. There are very dangerous forces at work." Rafe frowned, his fingers tightening around his glass. "But, I believe we've found a way to stop him. Unfortunately, it will take time. Time we may not have."

"Is there anything I can do to assist?"

"As much as it pains me to say, we could use the Navy of the Royal Court's help. Could you use your influence to have them step up patrols and strengthen defence of the coastal posts? It may not help, but it's something."

"I believe they'd be more than willing, considering

they just brought false accusations against you." Lord Merrill chuckled. "You are more than within your rights to take legal action against them, and I think it would not take much to enlist their cooperation with your efforts. In exchange for you overlooking their transgressions."

"Since I had no intention of pursuing the matter, by all means, trade my lack of reprisal for favours." Rafe grinned and gave a salute with his glass. "I do appreciate your assistance in all this."

"I'm the one who should be thanking you. We all should. Know that you have my prayers in this, a fervent wish of good fortune." Lord Merrill raised his glass and returned the salute. "Is there anything else I should know or assist you with?"

Rafe hesitated, unsure how the nobleman would answer if he would answer at all, but then asked, "What do you know of the Society of the Shadow Guard?"

"They're involved?" Lord Merrill nearly sputtered out a mouthful of port and then took a breath. "Not surprising though. They do seem to have an extraordinary amount of knowledge of all things magical."

"So you know of them? Who or what are they?"

"I've heard of them. They influence a great many circles I travel in, Captain, but not in a malevolent manner. As to who they are or what motivates them, I know little. I do know they have always protected the Kingdoms and the Islands, if from behind closed doors. But if they are involved, this matter may run far deeper and be far older than we suspected." Lord Merrill took another sip of port before finishing. "The Society of the Shadow Guard play the long game, Captain. Always the long game."

"I see. You think it best to accept their involvement, then?"

Lord Merrill nodded and a look passed between the two men. "You have little choice in that, I suspect, but you will receive no hindrance from them, only help."

Rafe smiled and raised his glass. "To help then, theirs and yours." He sipped his port, toasting his guest and all accords. He hoped it would be the forging of an alliance, borne on mutual understanding and a fine port.

A world away from wine and men, the darkness grew. Below the water, the dead stirred. Bones, picked clean by the fishes, twitched. Rotting corpses turned their ravaged faces towards the deeper depths. A beat drummed through the sea, *'Rise, Rise, Rise,'* shimmering against the remains of those drowned and claimed by the ocean. An answering moan sounded, ripped across the After World and through the water, a low wail of sacrilege and acquiescence, of new life thrust unwillingly on the dead. Disturbances rippled as they obeyed, crawling, swimming, drifting, sucked down, down into the maw of their new master.

The Terrible One watched, waiting for its offerings, its red eyes flickering raw with hunger, with salivating need. Its tentacles squirmed, crunching against the bones that made its bed, caressing the skeletons of the submissive slaves surrounding it. Its body moved in breath and power. Its mind alive in anticipated death.

Soon, soon. I grow stronger. Come to me, my legions, come. Feed me. Serve me. I am all. I will pick clean your bones, use you, destroy you! You are nothing. Your existence is nothing. You are mine. Mine! You are all mine! Come to me. Come to my eternal embrace.

Echoes of its thoughts snaked through the sea, seeping into the dark corners and the shadows of the worlds. Her shadows. Alone within her sanctuary, Bevire heard the bleak summoning and shivered. She clutched a black feather in her hand and took a deep breath. Bevire remembered the words of the Crow at their last meeting, the refrain of 'naughty, naughty' taunting her like she was a child. She heard the Crow's cruel laughter, felt the satisfaction of its scream when she yanked a feather from its wing and remembered the joy as she banished the creature from her realm.

"You think you are so clever, Crow, so clever. But I know a few tricks too. I have a name now, and this." She twirled a black feather against her fingers. "My fear started this, I will end it." She blew on the feather she held, whispering 'Ashetus' as she puffed swirls of night and magic into the strand of plumage. The feather wriggled and writhed, separating, duplicating until three feathers lay upon her palm. She smiled and reached into the air with her other hand. She plucked a filament of gloom from the shade of existence around her and bound it to the feathers. One breath, two breaths, her magic cascaded outward, stretching, forming the feathers and shadows into her will, into a weapon bonded to a whispered name. Within the space of worlds and ten heartbeats, she held salvation in her palm. She held one arrow, black as pitch and powerful enough to kill a beast as old as time.

Chapter Eleven

Old Mother Abel

"So do we trust him?" Blackthorne inquired of his captain, referring to Lord Merrill who was safely back on shore in Abersythe. The two of them stood together on the quarterdeck, Rafe finally above deck and talkative now that they were in sight of Outcast Key.

"Lord Merrill? I think we do trust him. He still has his secrets, I'm sure, but don't we all. And, for now, our interests align."

Blackthorne sighed. "That's good. We don't need more enemies, especially now. We left one at our back in Black Shoals and look to make another when we weigh anchor."

Rafe nodded. "I know. Pelham will have to wait for another day, but Mother Abel is not so much a fool as to make me her enemy. She'll growl and balk, but she'll cooperate if only to be rid of us."

"I hope you're right. That woman is trouble."

"We can handle trouble, and time is of the essence more than ever." Rafe shivered at the memory of what he felt coming out of the After World the night before. "Ashetus is growing his army."

Blackthorne fell silent and conversation ceased. Only the normal sounds of the ship heralded them into the port of Silver Haven, the only acknowledged settlement of Outcast Key.

Berthed in the harbour, Rafe and Blackthorne disembarked the ship issuing strict commands for the rest of the crew to remain on board and be vigilant. The Key was well-known for being a home to ruffians, pirates and criminals of all kinds.

The pair received stares and dirty looks as they strolled along the docks, making their way to the outskirts of town. More than a few men and women fingered knives on their belts, but one look from Rafe discouraged any further actions and they walked to Old Mother Abel's hut unscathed.

About five feet from her door, Rafe grabbed Blackthorne's arm and yanked him to an abrupt halt. "Wait. Something's not right."

The captain mustered a few strands of blue energy from his fingertips and flicked them across the air. They spiralled like arrows and then exploded in a shattering burst of light.

Blackthorne jumped. "What the damnation! Why did you do that?"

Rafe grimaced. "I didn't. There's a blocking spell across the path. It would have kicked us both back on our asses. I guess Old Mother Abel doesn't like unexpected visitors." Rafe summoned more magic. "It won't take but a moment to break it, though."

He let a ball of energy fly full force at the spell, and the two magiks crashed together in a spectacular miniature cataclysm of sparks, sizzle, and luminescence. When the light show faded, Rafe strode forward past where the spell had stood. Blackthorne hesitated and then dashed after his captain.

"So much for any element of surprise, sir."

Rafe growled. "Damn surprise and anything else. I'm tired of games and interference." He swiftly marched up the path to Mother Abel's door and pounded his fist against the wood. "Open up old woman! Your parlour tricks didn't work!"

Rafe's knock at the door was met with much banging from the interior of the home and the hoarse shout of 'Go away!'

Rafe pounded on the door again and yelled, "Open the door old woman, or I'll knock it down and you with it!"

A scream of 'Damnation!' and hurried footsteps was followed by the crooked door being yanked open. A short thin woman with one good eye and a scar over the other glowered at them before recognition dawned. "God of Souls!" She shook her fist under Rafe's nose and spat on the ground. "I'll not go with ye! You've no right to arrest me, so you can take your damnable ghosts and ghouls and be off with ye!"

"I'm not here for your sorry hide, Mother Abel. I'm here to do business." He pulled a pouch full of coins from his pocket. "I'll pay you for what I want and for your silence."

"Business? And why would I want your money?" She scowled at him even as she eyed the pouch. "You'll ruin my reputation, you will."

"You won't do wonders for mine either, you old hag. But you'll take the coin and give me want I seek. You have no choice."

"Oh, don't I? I can refuse you, same as any. What's a man like you going to do? You ain't no cutthroat."

"No, I'm not." Rafe leaned forward until they were face to face. "But I'm not a man either, old woman, and you'd best remember that. I can take everything from you, and I do mean everything." He summoned a touch of magic, lighting his eyes in blue sparks and tugging gently at her soul. Old Mother Abel gasped, her heart fluttering until Rafe let go.

She grated her teeth and stood her ground for a moment longer, before surrendering. She moved aside and ushered the men in with a, "Step lively and enter before someone sees you."

Once inside Rafe wasted no time. "We need a copy of the song, *The Path of Sorrows*. A full copy, no missing lyrics. We were told you have such."

For a moment she stared, a look of bewilderment etched on her face. Then she burst out laughing, bending over almost double in her glee. When her merriment ended, she wiped tears from her eyes and flopped in a rickety chair. "Well now, I didn't expect that. By damnation, I near forgot about that. They said you would come nosing about one day, looking for that song. Damnation. I'll finally get out from under the likes of them."

"The likes of whom?" Rafe asked, even though he felt he knew the answer.

"My business, not yours. Don't ask me what mischief I get up to, and I'll stay out of your troubles. Men like you don't go nosing about Outcast Key searching for songs without mischief behind it."

"No mischief, but you're right. It's nothing you want a part of old woman, and something you're safer far away from. Give us the song, take the gold, and nothing else need be said."

She tapped her fingers on the arm of the chair. "Fair enough." Then an odd look crossed her face. She rose to her feet and tottered to an old cabinet, opening a drawer on the left. "I've got something for you." She withdrew a dusty tin box and trudged back to her chair. "Give me a minute to sort through. Most of my old odds and sods are in this box." She shuffled papers, placing a few on her lap and generally rummaged around the box. A glint of something and a shiver in his blood caught Rafe's attention and he grabbed Old Mother Abel's wrist as she raised her hand.

"I don't go down that easily, old woman."

"Let go, you bastard! It's not what you think!" She kicked out at him and the tin box tumbled to the floor. She swung her other arm, but Blackthorne stepped in and restrained her, essentially pinning her to the chair.

While she squirmed and cursed, Rafe pulled the arm he held upward and forced her hand open. He plucked a red stone from her palm.

"Be careful with that!"

Rafe let her go and took a step back still holding the gem. She reached up and tried to snatch it, but Blackthorne pushed her back into the chair. She glared at the two of them.

Rafe returned her glare. "A Shadow Spirit? You like to play with dangerous things, don't you? What were you planning? To banish us to another realm? Or try and escape yourself?" He tossed the gem in the air before catching it and slipping it into his pocket.

Old Mother Abel bared her teeth. "Neither fool. I told you, that's for you. Same as that song you come for. Been waiting most of my life to give you the damn things and discharge my debt to that damnable Society." She gasped, and a hand flew to her mouth.

"So it was them!" Rafe grinned as Old Mother Abel glared.

"You never heard that from me, but yeah. They gave me the charge of keeping things 'til the day you came for 'em. Or rather, blackmailed me, the bastards. But, like you said, both of us needn't mind the particulars of how things came to be." She nodded, giving him a defiant look. "That there stone's for you. The Society said you'd be needing it, maybe. Though I don't know what for and didn't ask."

Rafe looked at the red gem. "I'm surprised you didn't use it by now. A journey stone like this, it would make a good escape plan or send a few enemies somewhere they'd rather not be."

Mother Abel snorted. "Don't think I didn't consider it. Would've got me out of a scrape or two over the years, being capable of travelling between places or sending people somewhere else. But you and I know it can only be used the once. Couldn't take the chance. You don't cross the wishes of some folks. You just don't." Mother Abel rose, keeping a wary eye on Rafe and Blackthorne. "But that ain't the prize you come for." She scurried to her cabinet and banged twice on the side on the oaken cupboard. A small, hidden drawer snapped open, and she plucked a folded, yellowed piece of paper from a bundle secreted within. Then she slammed the drawer shut.

"Here's a copy of the thing you seek, but I warn you, I never made much of it and I doubt it will be easy to find what you're looking for. And you'll be lucky to survive what needs doing, I'm guessing." She cocked her head as if waiting for an answer.

Rafe didn't reply, only held out his hand for the paper. She waved it before snatching it away with a smile. "Not yet. You promised coin, remember?"

"So I did." Rafe slid the pouch out of his pocket and offered it on an outstretched palm. Old Mother Abel did the same with the slip of paper, and both grabbed their respective rewards.

Rafe unfolded the parchment, read it, and sighed. She hadn't cheated him by the looks of it. He had the song. He had what he needed. It wasn't another trick.

"Don't trust me?"

"Of course not."

She cackled. "At least you have brains."

Rafe tucked the valuable song into his pocket. "We'll take our leave now. It hasn't been a pleasure." Both he and Blackthorne turned to go.

"Wait!" She licked her lips. "About the stone. If you don't use it, can I have it back?"

Rafe looked back. "Maybe, old woman. I may return the gem when this is over. If it is unused, that is."

"Fair enough. And if you're still alive to do anything, you bastard." She chuckled. "Off with you then, both of you, and don't set foot here again less you be returning the stone."

"Yes, ma'am." Rafe grinned. He opened the door to leave.

"Just one more thing, God of Souls." Rafe paused, his foot on the threshold and Blackthorne already out the door.

"Yes, old woman?"

"That ditty will only lead ye to the horn." She cracked a grin at his astonished look. "Of course I knew, ye fool. I never do nothing without knowing the whole of it." She cackled. "And they gave me one last message for you. If you want the bow, you'll need to go to Raven Rock. To the Grey Sisters. They're the ones I swore the oath to. They're the ones who guard the secrets of the bow. The Society answers to them."

With a sudden chill, Rafe walked out the door chased by her laughter. He and Blackthorne hurried on to their ship, glad to be rid of the woman.

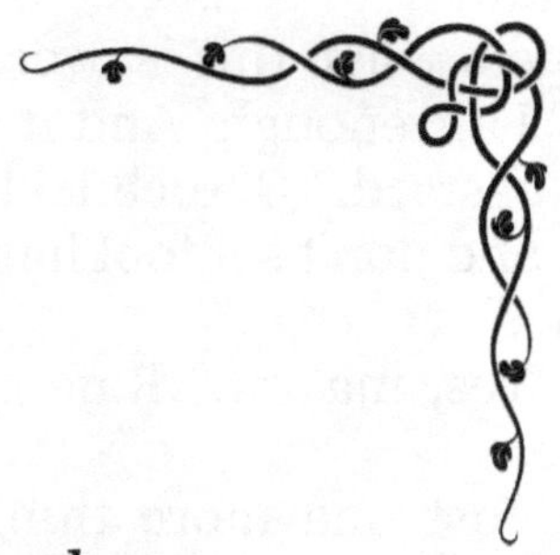

Chapter Twelve

To Raven Rock

Rafe sat alone in his quarters, Outcast Key behind them and the course to Raven Rock set. A disgruntled Blackthorne stalked the decks above him, keeping company with a grumbling crew. No one, including himself, felt at ease sailing to Raven Rock to see the Grey Sisters.

However, at that moment those worries were pushed aside as he studied the parchment and the strange words of *The Path of Sorrows*. He sighed, reading the words over again, the same words of his mother's lullaby.

Hush, hush, close your eyes,
Against the night.
Hush, hush, the stars will shine,
Against the night.

The horn will sound.
The bones will fall.
The Hunter stalks the Terror.

Against the night,

The bow will sing.
The beast will die,
Underneath the raven wing.

So, listen well, oh, brave new soul,
And stand against the night.
Find the horn, and find the bow,
Along the Path of Sorrows.

He sighed again, mumbling to himself as he continued to read.

"That part is recounting the history, I think, and this next bit...maybe it's an old reference...maybe to the channel between Raven Rock and Seadog Isle."

The brave will seek,
The brave will find,
And ward against the night.
In the deep, past the dawn,
Between the dog and raven.

Down and down,
And down you go.
To the Path of Sorrows.
Only the brave remain alive,
To chase that Path of Sorrows.

He shook his head, knitting his brow. He leaned back in his chair, still muttering, "It's this part I don't understand." He picked up the paper and stared at it reading the words aloud.

Sail the brave, sail the line,
In the shadow of the night,
Where the dead bones lie,
Beneath black sands,

Between the seven keys,
And a skull with many teeth.

"That sounds like Pirate Keys, sir."

Rafe looked up with a start to see Mouse standing in the open doorway.

"I knocked, but you didn't seem to hear." The lad looked contrite. "Didn't mean to eavesdrop, sir, but, begging your pardon, that sounds a lot like how smugglers used to refer to Pirate Keys."

"Excuse me? Smugglers?"

Mouse smiled. "Back in my day, when I was still alive, I did a stint aboard a smuggling ship. I expect you remember them days, back when the Seven Kingdoms went and shoved those taxes on all the good folk of the Islands?"

"I do, but was preoccupied with another matter during those months. I heard of the increase in smuggling, but can't say I paid much attention."

"Oh, it was a right lively trade back then, run out of Pirate Keys. How the place made its reputation. At least in part. Other things were going on in those islands too, which is why we all took to being cagey. You never knew who was listening back then. Take what you were reading. The main island down there is called Black Sand, and there is a little cluster of seven keys to the east of it. And we used to joke about the islands around Skull Reef, calling them its teeth."

"And 'where the dead bones lie?'"

"That's Shipwreck Cove. Sailors and smugglers alike used the saying, '*stay away from where the dead bones lie*,' for the island. On account of the pirates that lured in ships and wrecked them."

Rafe stared at Mouse and then at the paper. "That's it. Beneath, between, that's the location. You've solved it, Mouse. It's the Pirate Keys. Specifically Shipwreck Cove.

The horn is on Shipwreck Cove." Rafe grinned. "Have a seat lad and see what you can make of the last bit."

"Certainly, sir, but Commander Blackthorne did send me down here to check on you, sir. Shouldn't I be reporting back?"

"That can wait. In fact, if we puzzle this out, we can go up together. Now have a seat."

"As you wish, sir." Mouse crossed the room and perched gingerly on the edge of a chair. "What did you want me to puzzle?"

"This." Rafe picked up the paper and leaned back in his chair, reading aloud.

The storm will blow,
The bones will fall,
When the mouth of stone,
Shall open wide.

From the giant's maw,
Above the hand,
In the sky above the ruins.

Rafe looked at Mouse, who frowned. "Anything?"

"Don't know about a mouth of stone or a maw or hand, but there's a giant sure enough on Shipwreck Cove. A jut of land on the west side, a cliff called the Giant's Eye. Maybe if there's an eye, there's a maw and hand?"

"Perhaps. Nothing else comes to mind?"

"No, sir."

"Well, at least we have Shipwreck Cove as a starting point. And this Giant's Eye may prove worth looking at."

"As long as it doesn't look back, sir." Mouse grinned, and Rafe answered with a returned smile.

"I think we're safe on that account."

"So that's where we'll be headed then? After Raven Rock?"

"Most likely, unless the Grey Sisters shed more light on the whereabouts of the horn we're seeking. A dangerous journey I know, but we haven't any choice."

"I'd say more of a lark for this crew, sir, sailing through pirate territory. A bit less off-putting than monsters and goddesses, sir. And whatever else awaits us."

"I suppose that's true. Let's go report to Blackthorne, shall we, and tell him I have cause to stop brooding in my quarters." Rafe rose with a smile. "He should be thrilled to have something else to fret about other than me."

"I shouldn't think so, but he will be glad of a report." Mouse scrambled to his feet and fell into step behind Rafe as they left and made their way on deck. Blackthorne spied them as they emerged into the sunlight, the first mate standing at the edge of the quarterdeck, his hands on the railing, looking down.

"So you coaxed him from his den, Mouse. Good lad."

"He did more than that. He solved our conundrum of a riddle." Rafe grinned as Mouse blushed, the sailor retreating into the milling crew. The captain bounded up the steps and came face to face with his commander. "I know where to start looking for the missing horn."

Blackthorne stepped aside to allow Rafe to pass on to the upper deck. "Where, sir? Some black abyss full of bloodthirsty monsters? Would be along the lines of how our luck is running these days."

Rafe turned his head, still grinning. "Close. Pirate Keys."

Blackthorne raised an eyebrow. "Oh. Only cutthroats and pirates this time around. A quiet change of pace."

"That's what Mouse said. I'm glad you agree." Rafe teased, "We're due for a gentle peaceful trip."

Suddenly, as if in defiance of his very words, the sky rumbled in thunder across soft pale clouds and the bluest of sky. A fierce wave rolled under the Jewel tossing her like flotsam and creating a flurry of curses from the crew.

Another wave rolled, rocking the ship, and a familiar shriek echoed through the sky.

"Man your stations, men!" Rafe barked the command in his first breath after the sound. "Prepare for battle! Blackthorne take command! Hold the line!" The crew raced across the decks, swords in hand, ready for a fight. The clang of the ship's bell echoed through the rigging for what little protection it could offer.

Without further explanation, Rafe dashed off, weaving past his brave men, running below decks to his quarters. He yanked open a drawer and snatched up the stone he received from Mother Abel. Racing back above deck, he darted out as the cry of 'Rising bones' hit the air.

Rafe ran to the quarterdeck to witness the sea ascend in the distance, the wall of water holding an awful sight. Dozens of skeletons and half-rotted corpses rode the sea wave, embalmed in the water, writhing and groping in some twisted semblance of life. Above the unnatural tide of ocean, Sea Ghouls flew, and they all bore down on the *Jewel* in a screaming cacophony of death.

Rafe didn't hesitate, pouring his magic into stone and shouting, "Shadows of Spirits, Shadows of Worlds, be gone from this place! Back to the depths!"

A counteracting wave of magic shot outward, meeting the sea as it crashed into the ship. Screams of undead things shattered the air as water swamped the *Jewel,* and the ship careened, listed, and nearly capsized. Men shouted and tumbled, gear went flying, and pieces of bone bounced off the rigging while lines snapped and sails waved free.

Rafe fell to his knees as the vessel came about, One-Eyed Anders struggling at the wheel to hold her true. Rafe pressed his fingers against the deck, calming the ship, pouring magic into her timbers. She settled, her planks groaning, her rudder straining, but still afloat and in one piece. Wave and ghouls had vanished as well as corpses and skeletons, though the deck was littered with pieces of bone and flesh that the spell had missed.

Rafe looked around, his ship scattered with debris and drenched, his crew piled in battered heaps. He heard the sounds of moaning, but everyone looked ambulatory and relatively unhurt. Rafe glanced at Blackthorne who clung to the rail, water dripping from his brass buttons, and then at Anders who grasped the wheel in a pale death grip. He climbed to his feet and shouted, "Head count! We need a head count! Anyone overboard? Anyone injured?"

Rafe stumbled down to the lower decks, and Blackthorne scrambled to his feet, his boots squelching as he followed the captain. Through the puddles and the jumble, they took count and, thankfully, found not a soul lost if several suffering bumps and bruises. Those that could manned their duties and the ship began to hum in a mode of recovery.

"We've flooding below decks, but we won't sink, and we've lost a good third of the gear that wasn't tied down." Blackthorne's voice shook as did his hands, but Rafe let him speak. He seemed to need it. "There are dead bits and bones across the deck, but that will get cleaned, and the injured are being tended. Cuts, bruises, and a broken bone or two, though poor Red Wilson took a shard of bone in his arm. Sticking out right above the elbow. He's down below getting it extracted and the wound sewn up." Blackthorne took a breath, his demeanour slowly calming. "What was that, sir? I've never felt so..."

"Threatened, overwhelmed? Like you stared at impending death? I felt it too. The air felt heavy, dark as if the descending wave carried something—"

"Evil." Blackthorne finished his sentence, and Rafe nodded. The first mate cast his eyes around the ship, taking in the confusion and mess. "We were lucky, sir, weren't we?"

"Yes. If the stone hadn't banished the dead back into the sea, if they managed to attack...I hate to think of what we would have faced. We'll need that luck to hold to the end of this. We'll need that luck to hold."

Chapter Thirteen

The Grey Sisters

A sombre crew sailed into a sheltered cove and anchored off the island of Raven Rock. Men set to tidying the ship and fixing any remaining damage done by the thwarted attack, while Rafe and Blackthorne were rowed to shore in a jolly boat. The pair alighted on the sand, and Rafe dismissed the rest of the men.

"Go back to the ship. I'll send a signal when we're ready to return."

"If we return." Blackthorne's faint grumble fell on Rafe's ears only, and the captain gave him a sharp look. Blackthorne stared at the sand as the boat rowed away.

"You didn't have to come." Rafe watched the boat move off. "You could have stayed on the ship."

"No, sir." Blackthorne squared his shoulders. "It's just...this whole business doesn't sit right. Not only coming here. It feels like...like it's the end. As if, whatever happens, the world won't be the same."

"You do know I hate it when you get these premonitions, don't you?"

"I do, sir. I do."

A gust of wind blew sand between them, and the trees behind them rustled.

"Listen to your man, God of Souls. He is a perceptive one."

They turned to see three cloaked figures standing where the beach met the tree line. A breeze swirled around the trio, tugging at their grey cloaks, playing with wisps of their white hair. Silver eyes glinted under their hoods like stars surrounded by shadows, and their voices echoed together as they spoke once more.

"Welcome. We have been expecting you. We have the answers you seek, and more. Follow us."

Trees parted as if alive, revealing a path through the wooded area and underbrush. The three women glided forward, Rafe and Blackthorne hurrying along in their wake. They were led to a perfect circle of trees with cascading red leaves encasing a clearing. The women slipped between the vegetation into the glade. Blackthorne and Rafe hesitated at the edge of the woodland.

"Join us in the circle, gentlemen. Come, come."

Rafe took a breath and walked into the clearing, Blackthorne at his heels.

The women moved, forming a semi-circle in front of the two men. "We see between the worlds. We stand between the shadows and the stars." They pushed down their hoods, wild manes of white hair and haggard faces exposed to the day. Three sets of eyes stared at Rafe with something akin to amusement. "We have been waiting for this day. For this and other days." They laughed a cold, vibrating sound. "Your path is a long one, God of Souls, and you walk much of it blind. You seek for answers. You have questions. And always the maelstrom swirls around you as much as you try to escape."

Rafe gritted his teeth, his patience exasperated. "Enough with the vagueness. Can you help me? I need—"

The Grey Sisters cackled again, interrupting him. "We

know what you need. Do you? We saw you flailing here and yon. Following our clues. The trail of crumbs left for you. We know you seek the Horn of the Gods. We know you must retrieve the Bow of the Hunter." The trio snuffled half a snort, half a laugh. "And you do not need our help to find the path that leads to the horn. That journey has been revealed to you through a little shipboard Mouse."

Startled and angered by their unexpected reference, Rafe snapped, "What do you know of that? Have you been spying on me?"

The Grey Sisters chuckled. "We spy on everyone. Don't think you are special. How else do we know when the threads of destiny are coming to their place in time?"

"Destiny?" Rafe snorted. "Is that what you call all this twaddle? Hidden clues, cryptic babble, obscure hints to secret locations wrapped in a nonsense song? More like luck than destiny that I solved the puzzle at all."

"Perhaps." The Grey Sisters shrugged. "Or perhaps luck is just another word for destiny. The world is how you perceive it, God of Souls. And all destiny needs its keepers. Even if those keepers are sometimes poets that think they are clever." They sighed. "Sometimes we must make do with what we have and work to keep Fate on course. Even by spying."

Rafe frowned, not liking the implications of what they said. "How much have you been meddling?"

"As much as necessary. Don't be cross, God of Souls. Fate is nothing more than an alignment of happenstance. Sometimes, we must nudge such events to put everything in their place." They grinned. "So, whether by luck or meddling, you come to where you need to be. Does it truly matter how?" The wind gusted as they spoke, swirling the edges of their capes and scattered bits of vegetation.

Rafe stared, spitting a retort. "Who are you to play with the existence of the world and my life?"

"We are the Society of the Shadow Guard." The voices

of the Grey Sisters turned grim and harsh, and the air lost its warmth. "We are the Keepers of Harmony against Chaos. We stand against forces older than the creation of this mortal world in a cause you barely comprehend."

Rafe stood his ground even as his skin shivered but said nothing in reply. For a moment, they glared at each other, and then the Grey Sisters smiled. They spoke softly, gently. "You have what you need, however the cause. Stop fussing over the delivery. Petulance will gain you nothing."

Rafe sighed, still angry, but gave ground. They were correct. He nodded his compliance.

"Good. Now you must act and sail your path for soon there will be need of the Horn. The bones are coming, rising to drag the living into the dark, deep sea." This time the Grey Sisters shivered as a cold wind blew across the glade. "Travel the course you set, and the horn will be revealed by the Giant's Eye."

A trickle of lingering annoyance mixed with unexpected relief slid along the edge of his thoughts, and Rafe sucked in a breath. He let it out slowly, asking, "What of the bow?"

The three women smiled. "Our secret. One that comes with a price." They all raised a hand and pointed at Rafe. "The price of a promise. The Hunter's Bow is yours for a promise." A silence settled over the glade. All movement, all sound ceased.

Rafe felt his magic stir in his blood as if he stood on the edge of something remarkable...or terrible. When he answered the sisters, his voice came out a whisper. "What promise?"

"To return here when you have retrieved them. Return here with the bow and the gift. Here at Raven Rock is where the beast must be summoned to this world. Here is where it will be killed. You must bring your army to the island. Your soldiers will meet his in these waters. Only here he can die. We have seen this, and you must promise."

Rafe stared at them. "What are you talking about? I

don't have an army."

"You will." The sisters nodded in unison. "You will. They will come to you after she brings the gift. Promise us, and you will have the bow."

Rafe licked his lips, confused but willing. He inhaled and said, "I promise."

"Welcome to the first step of a greater destiny, God of Souls." Their high-pitched laughter broke the quiet, and the sky erupted in thunder. "The bow lies with the girl who sees, underneath the temple rock she rules: an Oracle's chamber underground marked by your Sign of the Star."

"What?" The witches' words took him aback. "Are you talking about the old passages beneath Rock Island Temple?"

The witches nodded.

Rafe stared, his mouth open. "That's impossible. The temple may be old, but it's not that old."

"Of course not. Your Temple is merely the last place the Bow has rested. A whisper here, a twitch there, and the Horn and Bow fade in and out moving between time. The Society sees to that." The three women smiled. "Now you have your answers. Seek the Horn first. It will be needed soon. Then the Bow to end the beast."

They moved together and glided past Rafe and Blackthorne. "That is all you require this day. We await your return. Now come with us back to the beach."

They slid through the trees, leaving Rafe and Blackthorne no choice but to follow them.

Once back to the shore, Rafe tossed a ball of energy into the sky, a burst of magic to signal the jolly boat to return. Blackthorne walked to the water's edge, leaving him alone with the Grey Sisters. He stared, words on the edge of his lips. About the Society, his family, and so much more.

The women smiled, shaking their heads. "Save your questions. We will not answer. But we will tell you this.

You walk between worlds, God of Souls. Between the Stars and the Night, between the Living and the Dead. Never fully of one, yet dwelling in all. We do not envy you." A strange pitched cackle sounded in unison from the trio, and Rafe repressed a shudder.

Then he gave a nod, his queries unspoken, and a reply, "Not a sentiment I am unfamiliar with, good ladies. I doubt you'd find a soul in any world that would envy me."

Another cackle and they said, "You might be surprised, God of Souls. Indeed, you might be surprised." The three gave a final laugh and wandered back into the trees leaving Rafe to stare at their retreating backs. He turned to Blackthorne as he felt a hand on his shoulder.

"Time to go, Captain."

"Indeed." They walked back to the water's edge to wait for the jolly boat.

⁕

Rafe stood on the quarterdeck watching the ship cut through the waters, sailing away from Raven Rock. On either side stood Mouse and One-Eyed Anders, Blackthorne at the helm.

"Well, gentlemen, you two seem to be our resident authorities on where we're headed. What's our best course through the Pirate Keys to Shipwreck Cove?"

"The lad and I have been discussing it, sir, and it seems keeping to the edge of the seven unnamed keys, sailing through their channels, putting them between us and Black Sand Island would be best. If we come in along the backside of Shipwreck Cove, out of sight of Black Sand, we look to avoid the worst of them pirates."

"Sounds reasonable. What do you think Blackthorne?" Rafe turned to his first mate.

"Avoiding pirates sounds very reasonable to me."

"Then a winding sail through the seven keys and the backside of Shipwreck Cove it is. But we'll man the cannon and the harpoons and set watch for marauding ships. Blackthorne, relinquish the wheel to Mr. Anders if you would and ready the ship."

"Aye, Captain." Blackthorne handed off the helm and walked to the lower deck while Anders eased the ship out to open water.

"Set the course, Mr. Anders."

"Aye. Setting course, Captain. Straight to Pirate Keys."

Chapter Fourteen

Pirate Keys

The *Jewel* sailed into the Keys undetected, winding through the islands with shipboard tensions high and every sailor on alert. Not until they turned to exit their sheltering lee and tack around Shipwreck Cove did they find trouble.

The cry came from the spotters in the rigging. "Two ships dead ahead! Flying the Sword and Skull on their mast!"

"Are they moving towards us or blocking the channel?" Rafe shouted as he raised his spyglass to scan the horizon. Sure enough, he spotted two distinctive pirate flags waving in the distance.

"Blocking the port side of the channel, Captain! Trying to herd us, I think!"

"Sounds like they be trying to drive us round Shipwreck Cove into the rocks, Captain. Or to Black Sand and their waiting ships at Deadhead Cove." One-Eyed Anders jumped into the conversation as Rafe confirmed the other ships' positions through his spyglass.

"It seems so, Mr. Anders. Bring the ship port side and aim her between the ships. We'll show those pirates that we can't be herded like cattle!" To the rest of the crew, he shouted, "Full sail! Maintain speed!"

Blackthorne shot him a worried glance. "What are you planning, sir?"

Rafe grinned. "Do you remember Cockcrow Bay?"

"I do." Blackthorne groaned and then whirled, shouting down to the main deck. "Man the guns, boys! Captain's going to try the Starburst maneuver! If they don't run, we may be engaging the enemy!"

Rafe trotted to the far end of the quarterdeck and turned to face the bow of the ship. With his back against the stern, he grabbed hold of the outside rail with both hands, summoned his magic and ignited the corresponding power of his ship. He felt the hum of energy that snaked through the wood, the cadenced shuddering of the rudder, the thwack of the sails in the wind, the power running like lifeblood through the grain and fibre of the *Jewel*.

He connected to it, awakened the bond that held them together, made his magic and hers one. He focused their energy, controlled it, waited until the striking moment, and sent it barrelling through the ship on a stream of shining sea-blue energy. The blast shot straight out the prow into the sky and streaked across the air like lightning. It smashed into one of the pirate ships, shattering the foremast and leaving a smoking hole in the deck. Another blast followed, smashing into the other ship before Rafe collapsed to his knees, his heart racing, his breathing rapid.

Cheers echoed over the ship and shouts of, "They're turning tail!" washed across deck.

Rafe leaned against the railing, croaking out the words, "Maintain the guns and the watch and our speed. Full sail." Blackthorne relayed the quiet commands with barked orders, and the crew cut short their jubilation for duty. To Anders, the captain said, "Set our course around the island. Get us about Shipwreck Cove to the Giant's Eye." Then he leaned back against the rail and closed his

eyes to rest.

"Done with your nap, sir? We've arrived."

The voice woke Rafe who still sat on the quarterdeck. He scrambled unsteadily to his feet as Blackthorne repeated what he said.

"We've arrived at the Giant's Eye."

Rafe looked out to see a beach and an island cliff off the starboard side of the ship. Vegetation, crags, and trees dotted the spit of land and the towering edifice, but a great outcropping could be clearly seen in roughly the shape of an eye.

Rafe tugged at his coat, straightening the seams, ignoring the fact he fell asleep on deck. "So it seems. And now that we have an eye, are there any indications of anything else? Features or stones that resemble a mouth or hand?"

"No sir, but we haven't gone in too close as the waters around here can be shallow according to Mouse. We did spot some remains of what looks to be a crumbled structure. Possibly a shrine. Whatever it used to be, it is old."

Rafe inhaled and whispered, "In the sky above the ruins."

"Excuse me, sir?"

"A line in the song. Where did you find this old shrine?"

"Inland from the beach, half-covered by the underbrush." Blackthorne handed Rafe a spyglass. "Look a bit to the east, under the cliff edge."

Rafe looked out studying the island shoreline. He soon spotted the remains of an ancient structure poking out of the island foliage. "How are the waters? Good enough to take a smaller boat to shore?"

"Yes, sir. A jolly boat can land without an issue or a longboat if you want a larger landing company."

Rafe lowered the spyglass. "A longboat. We'll need several men to properly search the ruins."

"Aye, captain." Blackthorne barked orders, and the crew manned the winches hauling the longboat into position to lower into the water. Shouts, squeals, and creaks filled the ship as the first mate turned back to Rafe. "Who do you want going ashore with you?"

Rafe considered his options and then replied. "Striker Angus, Short Davy, Pinky Jasper, Josiah Collins, and fill the rest of the places with our best oarsmen. I want you to remain on the ship in case any marauders come sniffing around and maintain the guns at the ready."

Blackthorne nodded and walked down to the main deck to inform the men. Rafe hesitated for a moment, still slightly unsteady before following.

Half an hour later, the longboat was in the water and rowing ashore. When they hit the beach, the men disembarked and hauled the longboat up the sand, past the tidemark. Then they milled around the captain awaiting their orders.

"Angus, you lead the trek inland. With your sense of direction, we'll make good time. The rest of us, a single file march to the ruins. And keep your eyes open. The place looks deserted, but, in the Pirate Keys, you never know."

Striker Angus pulled out his compass from his coat pocket and took bearings. "It's this way," pointing in a northeasterly direction.

"Onward then, men!"

With the captain's words, they set off inland.

After a twenty minute slog through the overgrown brush, trees and tangled vines—hacking the worst of it with swords—they stumbled upon a jumbled pile of stones. A few more steps past a thicket of trees revealed a foundation wall and other broken bits of structure including a crumbling arch. Angus held up a hand signalling a stop.

"We're here, sir. Now what?"

Rafe walked over beside Angus. "Now we search." He turned slightly and shouted. "Fan out! Comb the ruins for symbols, writings, hidden spaces, anything that looks off or odd, but don't stray too far afield. And try to keep in sight or shouting distance of each other."

A scurry of footsteps headed into the ruins, leaving Rafe standing alone looking upward. The cliff towered above the deteriorated archway, the Giant's Eye staring out at the horizon. He frowned. This close to the cliff face it seemed different, more rounded. Rafe shrugged and joined the others in the search.

Another twenty minutes later, he was sweating, frustrated, and tired of staring at vine-meshed stone. Then a shout rose from nearer the archway under the cliff face.

"Sir! This might be something!"

Rafe followed Short Davy's voice and found the man kneeling, tugging vegetation away from pieces of broken stone. More ripped up plant material lay nearby.

"What have you found?"

"It's a brazier, sir. Half covered by this ruin. This debris may be what's left of an altar fire pit. I think this broken wall is part of a chimney." Davy tapped on a rectangular length of masonry. "I've seen similar structures on Shadow Cay where I grew up. They're used for prayers and offerings to the gods." Davy grinned. "I'm thinking maybe that eye on the cliff was symbolic of whoever they worshipped here, 'cause I found something else too." He brushed away the last of the plant growth. "Writing, sir. It's faint, but you can make out an engraved inscription. Can't read it though. Looks familiar, but it's no language I know. Thought maybe you might know?"

Rafe crouched down and peered at the worn markings. "This is interesting." He ran his finger lightly against the rock with surprise. "It's Chynguri. A script based on the first language of Odiki used solely in the early shrines, solely to talk to the gods."

"What does it say, sir?"

We offer our breath to the stars. May the smoke from our fire and the prayers from our hearts reach the guardian. With the hand of offering, we light the way. May he grant protection. May he inhale our breath and our prayers, and may we become one.

Rafe looked up, imagining the path of ancient smoke. Directly above him loomed the Giant's Eye. "Odd that. They keep mentioning breath, and yet..."

Davy craned his neck, casting his gaze upward with Rafe's. "Maybe they saw something different up there than we do." The sailor shrugged. "Maybe something's changed."

"Maybe." Rafe mused, an idea forming. He made a quick decision. "Round up the men and wait for me here."

He scrambled to his feet and took a step back. He summoned his magic and slowly rose into the air.

He floated into the sky effortlessly, leaving a soft trail of blue wisps ascending far above the trees until he was level with the Giant's Eye. As he moved in closer, he saw the shape of the rock formation, an overhanging and ledges encasing a deep crevice in the cliff. In addition, he saw— while easily imagined as an eye shape—that the formation could also pass as a mouth.

Rafe moved his fingers, conjuring strands of energy. He flicked them into the air, shifting them across the wind into the darkness of the fissure. They twirled inside, lighting the interior in azure radiance. Rafe peered into the interior of the rock. Nestled within the dim core, rested a grey stone box.

Rafe leaned forward and reached his arm inside. He clutched at the top of the box, tugging it slowly from the hole in the cliff until he could grab it in both hands and extract it. It felt lighter than he expected, and, upon quick examination, he saw the construction was of porous stone.

He whispered, "Mermas. They used to make reliquaries

from this stone." Rafe ran his fingers around the box feeling a seam and a small indentation on one side, but no keyhole or lock. He tried prying off the lid, but it refused to budge. Rafe tucked the box under his arm and descended to the ground.

"You found it!" A jubilant cry came from Davy, and the rest of the men cheered.

"I found something." Rafe tempered the celebration, but still grinned, holding out the container on display. "Now we have to figure out how to open the box. I tried lifting the cover, but it won't be that easy it seems."

Davy stepped forward, tilting his head to study the object. "No hinges or latch on this side or the ends. Anything on your side, sir."

"Just an indentation."

"Did you try pressing it in? Like them puzzle boxes they sell in the Gallford marketplace."

"Worth a try." Rafe placed his thumb on the depression in the stone. It felt warm under his skin and it tingled. He pushed inward. A faint click sounded and then a succession of three more snaps. He pulled at the lid and it came off with ease. "Well, Davy, it seems you are the man of the hour."

Rafe showed the box, revealing a grey hunter's horn inside. "We found our first prize, men. We may win this battle yet." He grinned and replaced the cover on the box. "Let's get this treasure back to the ship, shall we?"

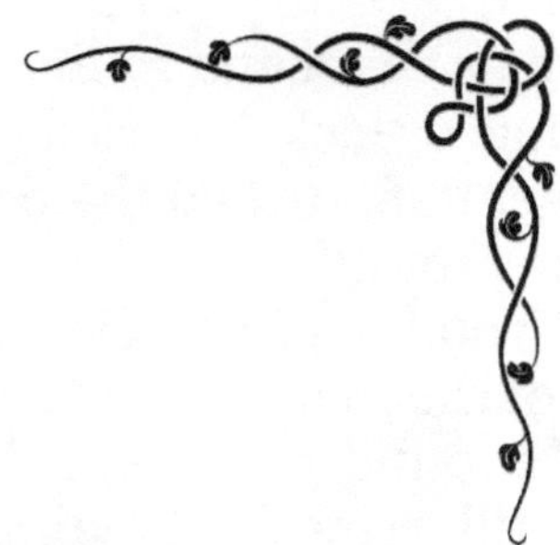

Chapter Fifteen

Into Darkness

A large black bird watched a fading sun perched on a pitted hunk of rock hewn by the sea and wind. With the sunset dancing colours over his plumage, the Nightmare Crow sat alone nursing his anger and a sore wing. He sensed the world turning along his schemes, breaking to the ending he desired.

"Pawns and more pawns though they think they are kings and gods. They are small. With petty minds. Darkness and life, worlds and realms, it is all nothing. They have never seen what matters. They do not know." He cawed and cackled, the sound rippling off the waves and the silent air. "She thinks she knows, plucking feathers. Feathers, feathers, she is still my pawn. And it all plays towards the endgame. My endgame. And my prize. I shall have it all!"

The bird shifted his weight and spread his wings ignoring the twinge of pain. "Do you hear me Terrible One? Ashetus, down in your stinking dark, deep hole! Crush your bones and strip bare the poor dead fools you consume! I do not care! Ravage the whole world. It is naught to me! You will rise, and you will fall! You will be the sacrifice! He is not the Hunter!"

The sea beneath the tiny spit of an island rumbled, and the wind moaned in the agonized cries of the dead. The crow laughed.

"Shake your fist, oh Terrible One, and make your threats. It is nothing to me! I know you. I know your weakness. I have planned and whispered and watched, long, long years. I thought to peck out your eyes myself, but this will have to do. I will see my revenge. I have not forgotten, Ashetus! I have not forgotten!"

The Nightmare Crow leapt into the air, wings spread soaring into the clouds, its shrieking voice falling back beneath the sea.

"I have not forgotten!"

The voice of the Crow descended, sinking deep, deep, past the sea, beyond the diaphanous weave between realms. It shattered against bones, and rebounded off unseen walls, stirring dreadful memories. Ashetus howled, tentacles lashing out, smashing skeletons to powder, its teeth gnashing the corpses hanging from its mouth to dust.

I killed them! Killed them! Shadow Birds! Shadow Birds! Why didn't they die? Kill the birds! Kill the birds!

It rolled over, crushing the remains of five of its slaves, and pulverizing half of its bed of bones. Tentacles waved in the air as it thrashed at imaginary birds

Away, away! Stop pecking at me! It hurts! It hurts! The light! It hurts! No one will make me bleed! I kill! Not birds!

Ashetus roared, causing everything around him to splinter into shards and dust. The sound cracked through every world, shaking the foundations from bedrock to the stars. Sea waves smashed against coastlines, mountains trembled, and the gods cried out. The ripples confounded every living creature and every soul in the After World.

Tears came unbidden, and prayers were offered by even the most undevout. Death herself quivered.

Ashetus noticed none of it. It wailed until its memories faded and then blinked its eyes.

Black bird. Black Crow. I remember you. I remember you. You left. You hated. You will die. You will die slowly.

Bevire clutched the arrow and shuddered. In her sanctuary, she felt the roar of Ashetus. Her magic wavered, and, for a moment, she lost sight of her brother's ship. The viewing portal she conjured shimmered, threatening to slam shut, but she yanked the shadows back open. She saw the sea toss the *Jewel* like a twig on a river, and the ship fight to stay steady. A cry caught in her throat until the world and the water calmed. She sighed, relieved, but still afraid. She kept watch until the ship sailed away from Pirate Keys, headed back to the Outer Islands.

"He found it. We have a chance." She stroked her arrow. "Time to leave. Time to go into the mortal world. My brother needs his gift."

Chapter Sixteen

The Horn of the Gods

"It doesn't look like much, sir." Blackthorne wrinkled his nose. "It's hand carved, to be sure. Bone or porous stone?" The pair sat in his quarters assessing the horn as the ship sailed out of the Pirate Keys headed for Rock Island.

Rafe turned the horn over, inspecting the object carefully. "Not bone, but not stone either. At least no stone of this world. I've seen something made of similar material, something my father owned. But you are right about one thing. It's not a very attractive thing."

He put the horn on his desk and stared at it. Maybe three hand spans long and tapered with the larger end curving into a bell shape, the object was a plain dull grey and scarred in carving marks. It bore no decoration and engraving and seemed more the sort of thing used by shepherds than gods.

Still...there was something about it that called to his blood.

"I don't think this horn is from the world of mortals, my friend. I'm not sure it's even from the world of the gods.

It doesn't feel like my magic, but there's power there. Like it's buried in the substance it's made from, buried in the thing itself."

"Do you think it will work? Drive off what's rising from the sea? If what happened off Shipwreck Cove is any indication, we haven't much time left. I'm just glad you were back on board with this," he nodded at the horn. "When that sea wave hit."

"Yes. We may have struck a nerve retrieving our prize. And it is a prize, but what kind I'm not sure. It's powerful, that I know. How I cannot say yet, but if I can focus its power, then yes, we may have a chance. But I'll feel better when we have the bow in our hands as well."

"So would I. We're hitting top speed straight to Rock Island. Even without you adding magic into the mix, the ship is shedding distance as if she knows the urgency."

"She does. Everything in the magic realms does. That... that happening, as you put it, was not ignored. Ashetus offered up a challenge. I'd expect fear and chaos greeting us on our return."

"As if we didn't have enough problems."

"Indeed. Expect a rough journey, old friend, even if seas be good for sailing."

Far away from Rafe's words, the predictive intent of them unfolded. As per Lord Merrill's promise, the Navy of the Royal Court patrols increased and regularly sailed around the islands. Assigned the Black Shoals to Tenby Key patrol, Commander Pelham stood on the quarterdeck of his ship, *The Sea's Favour,* scanning the horizon with his spyglass. Beside him stood his trusted first mate, Lieutenant Commander Francis Montague.

"It's an affront, Montague, an affront to decency and order. The scoundrel, Morrow is out chasing phantasms in some cockeyed notion of ancient monsters while we've been demoted to patrol duty. And worse, patrols ordered on his say-so by that...that...by Lord Merrill." Pelham clenched his jaw, lowering the spyglass. "It's hysteric nonsense inspired by a story from a shipwrecked sailor. The *Coral Rose* was most likely attacked by pirates or run aground by a drunken crew. This is why Captain Morrow has to go. He and his magic. He relies on old beliefs, superstition, and gibberish to manipulate his doddering betters and the gullible masses."

"Aye, Commander." Montague nodded, folding his arms and looking dour. "He is no better than a pirate, he is. I've long thought Captain Morrow a rogue."

"Yes. A rogue. That's what he is. Spreading tales of god-like monsters, indeed." Pelham sniffed. "Sea beasts perhaps, but I think he exaggerated that threat. His words are all false rumours and lies."

A grumble came from the helm and the faint murmur. "False only if you ignore facts and the strange happenings of late."

"What was that, midshipman?" Pelham snapped his attention to the helmsman.

"Nothing, sir, begging your pardon, sir, just musing to myself." The sailor went red and prayed not to be reprimanded.

"That had better be all it is. I want no talk of that peculiar, but natural phenomenon. A rumbling of the earth it was. Nothing more. A rare occurrence, but it happens."

"Yes, sir. If you say so, sir."

"He does!" Montague barked at the helmsman, "And see you keep a silent tongue in your head! Eyes front and focus on your duty!"

The midshipman nodded and stayed quiet.

Pelham sighed and continued with his rant. "See how Morrow's lies infect the Islands. Even into the Navy of the Royal Court. Our men should know better, but the superstition still takes hold. That's why it galls me that my plan failed, Montague. It galls me. And now I have endangered my position at the fort. Forced to do patrols in his name."

"Aye, sir, it's vexing. But the Commodore said the duty was temporary, and you still are technically in command of the fort's navy."

"A command now overseen by the Commodore. As if I was a lowly ensign on probation." Pelham grimaced. "How did I come to this insufferable position? How did Morrow wiggle away? I was sure we had him. We had our justice."

"I don't know, sir. I surely don't." Montague shook his head. "But his luck can't hold forever. This latest escapade could be his undoing. When all these patrols and general alarm are shown to be an empty fool's errand."

"An excellent point, Montague. This could be the misstep we need to crush him." Pelham smiled. "We must make plans, prepare a strategy for—"

"Wave dead ahead!" A cry came from a spotter. "The sea's arising from the depths!"

"What!" Pelham screamed in outrage and raised his spyglass. "Nonsense! I will not tolerate such—" The remainder of his ire fell dead silent, replaced with the frantic shout of, "Hard to port! Hard to port!"

The startled midshipman yelped, but reacted to the command and yanked the wheel. The ship lurched, turning violently and listing against the waves as it sliced through the water. Sailors lost footing, tumbled bruised and cursing, and the bones of the ship groaned under the strain. Then all thoughts of aches and bumps disappeared as every pair of eyes gaped starboard.

In the distance, the sea rose seven feet straight up in a giant wave, a solid wall of water moving west. This vast swell of ocean groaned and wailed, and a chorus of guttural echoes cascaded across the sky. For trapped within the surge were living bones and corpses, dozens of reanimated remains of the dead. Misshapen, bunched together skeletons and decomposing bodies squirming and thrashing, swept along in the momentum of the wave. Their clacking remains created a perverse rhythm, a drumbeat sounding under their strident cries.

Every tongue on the *Sea's Favour* remained silent as if the monstrosity they witnessed stole their voices. Only the creak of the ship and the smack of the waves against her sides could be heard across the vessel with the sound of death in the distance. The sailors watched as the moving tide of water and bones passed, becoming smaller and smaller on the horizon.

Then the harsh voice of Montague finally broke the silence. "It's heading in the direction of Crickwell."

Those words revived Pelham, who had stayed immobile through it all, his disbelief crashing into real proof. "If that hits land..." A fear sliced through him. "Helmsman, change course! Turn about and head for Crickwell Island!"

To the rest of the crew, he shouted. "Full sail men! Man the rigging! I want top speed! Lay in a pursuit course of that..." He gritted his teeth and spit out. "That thing!"

Under his breath, he added, "May the gods help us."

Rafe paced the length of the decks from the bow to the stern, weaving in among the crew, muttering, carrying the Horn of the Gods. His mood had changed back to foul and unpredictable in the time spent racing to reach Rock Island.

"Not much longer. Crickwell Island to the port side. Not much longer." He kept saying the words over and over as he hit the steps to the quarterdeck for the third time in an hour and climbed.

Blackthorne fell in pace beside him as Rafe circled the upper deck. From the helm, Anders glanced over, and he and Blackthorne exchanged a look. The first mate took a breath and asked, "What's wrong, sir?"

"Everything. Nothing. Maybe something in-between." Rafe answered without breaking stride. "I don't know if we're too late or too early, but something's not right. Yet something is right. I feel like we're being moved across the game board to where we're supposed to be." He stopped abruptly, whirling to face Blackthorne who stood mere inches from his face. "Something's coming, or we're coming for something." He held up the horn. "We're going to need this sooner than I'd hoped." He then continued pacing, moving back down to the lower deck. On the quarterdeck, he left Blackthorne shaking his head and Anders remarking, "Well, that cleared matters up, didn't it?"

Rafe ignored them both, the sound of his footsteps on the boards filling his ears and worry filling his thoughts. The hum of the ship vibrated through the soles of his boots into his blood, and the air seemed to scream.

He stopped. The screams were real. There was a shrieking sound carried on the wind. He looked up to see the *Jewel* sailing around White Fin Point, coming into view of the southern shore of Crickwell Island and Sunlight Bay.

As they cleared the point, they sailed directly into chaos. The Sunlight Bay shoreline was flooded, a mass of destruction with a naval ship beached in the shallows. Swarms of screaming skeletons attacked the vessel, tearing, biting, smashing at the ship and the few sailors that seemed to remain onboard. On the sands, more of the ship's company fought to survive against another onslaught of dead men's bones. In the deeper waters of the cove, two additional naval ships fired their cannon into the surrounding shoreline trees and on tidal waves of the dead that rose from the bay.

"Turn the ship!" Rafe's command was immediate. "Take her into the battle!"

He dashed the length of the *Jewel*, heading to the bow as his crew rushed to duty. They raced into the bay at top speed, Rafe standing against the rail, the sleek taper of the prow stretching out before him.

He closed his eyes and lifted the horn to his lips. He inhaled and blew a magic-tinged breath into the mouth of the Horn of the Gods.

The instrument vibrated in his hand, a long strident note smashing its way out like the first boom of a furious thunderstorm. Rafe opened his eyes to see a wave of golden ripples shatter into the air and heard a repeated staccato harmony roar across the space between the *Jewel* and the battle in the bay. The surge of tone hit the combat like a punch, rattling the bones, and knocking sailors off their feet. Skeletons screeched, thrashing and gyrating as if pain, breaking off from any attack.

Rafe sounded the horn again, and again the smashing tide of sound crashed into the attacking army of bones, this time bringing them to their knees. With bloodcurdling wails, they stumbled, fell, and launched themselves into the water as waves reached up to pull them into the bay and then out to sea. In minutes, not a walking corpse remained only broken ships and injured naval sailors. Rafe scanned for signs of bodies, but of those, none could be seen. He didn't know if that was an indication of no fatalities or a sign of a horrible fate for the battle's dead.

He sighed and looked at the horn. "At least we know you work." Without turning, he shouted back a command, "Take us into the bay! Past the vessels that are still afloat and close enough to render aid to the beached ship and those ashore!"

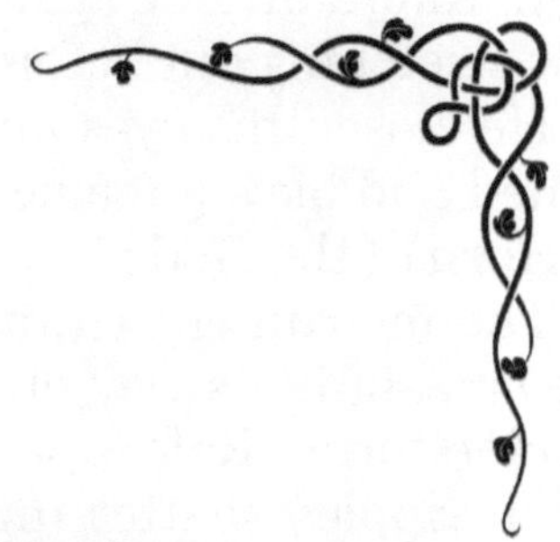

Chapter Seventeen

Tide of Invasion

Rafe stood on the shattered deck of the *Sea's Favour*. Two of her masts were snapped in half, her sails hanging in tatters, and she listed at an angle on the rocks, a gash torn in her hull, water partially flooding the lowest two decks. Not a sailor on board escaped injury with only a few still ambulatory and most in grave condition. Rafe's men and naval officers from the other two ships tended to them as well as to the injured men on shore in the distance. Rafe's gaze swept up towards the quarterdeck seeing Pelham kneeling on the boards, holding the still form of Lieutenant Commander Francis Montague. Rafe climbed the steps to the upper deck.

Commander Pelham glanced up, his face haggard and bleeding. "They tried to take him. Tried to drag his body into the sea after they killed him. Drove one of their broken bones right through his heart."

Rafe could see the long shard of bone still protruding from the Lieutenant Commander's chest and the expansive red stain on the dead man's uniform. Staring down, all he could feel was sorrow and pity. "I'm sorry."

Pelham laughed a harsh, hysterical sound full of pain and fury. "They tried to take him. But I wouldn't let them. I wouldn't let them."

Rafe knelt and put a gentle hand on Pelham's shoulder. "You did well by him, Commander. He was a brave man. He deserved better."

"He was. A brave man. I wouldn't let them take him."

"Yes. And they're gone now. You can let go and let us help. Get him home for burial and you some medical aid." Rafe signalled to men below. "Time to see to your ship, sir."

Pelham looked up confused. "My ship? My ship is done for, run aground. The crew, dead."

"No, sir. She's still clinging to life, battered and bruised, but still in need of you."

"My ship?" He looked bewildered for a moment as men filed past Rafe waiting for orders. Pelham seemed to notice them and squared his shoulders. "My ship needs me. My men must have a commander."

Pelham gently laid Montague on the deck boards and rose shakily to his feet. Rafe gave a surreptitious nod, and the body was tended to and covered with a cloth shroud. Pelham seemed pleased with the gesture.

"You take care of him. He will have a proper burial, laid to rest by his family." Pelham took a step towards the stairs and stumbled. Rafe moved, catching him before he fell. Pelham let out a cry.

"Are you injured, Commander?"

"Just my arm. They bit me, tore it up, but nothing that won't heal. Got knocked about a bit. Hit my head, but I smashed one of the blighters into pieces, I did."

"Good for you. But you should still have it looked at." Rafe coaxed him into sitting down on the steps. One of the medics came over to examine him, helping Pelham off with his coat.

"The commander is right. It's not bad, but I'll have to

clean it and stitch him up."

Rafe nodded. "Do it."

As the medic swabbed the wounds with a liberal dousing of alcohol, Pelham babbled amid winces of pain. "We gave chase, you know, and sounded the alarm. Our spellcaster is one of the best. Or perhaps was. I don't know whether he survived." Pelham hissed, either from the memories or the medical treatment, Rafe couldn't tell.

"They rose out of the sea and sailed past us, so we gave chase. They had swamped the island already. I sounded the order to storm the bay firing all guns. How was I to know?" He stared at Rafe, a remembered horror written on his face.

"Know what, Commander?"

"That there were more underneath us. Waiting. It was an ambush. The water surged below and slammed us onto the rocks. Just like the *Coral Rose*. Just like the *Coral Rose*." Pelham suddenly reached out and snatched at Rafe's sleeve, gripping the cloth tight. "You were right, Captain. You were right."

He let go and dropped his hand, crying out slightly as the stitching needle pierced his skin. "It was finished for us after that. Finished. We'd all be dead if the other ships hadn't arrived. If you hadn't arrived." Pelham closed his eyes and leaned his head against the stair railing, groaning as the needle and thread sewed up his wounds.

Rafe left him to the ministrations of the medics and his own haunting memories, walking back down to the lower deck. He found Blackthorne waiting for him.

"Word's come in, sir, passed along by spellcaster to one of the other navy vessels here, the *Star Defender*. There have been other attacks in and around Crickwell Island, Shadow Cay and Tenby Key. Even some places along the main peninsula coast. Navy ships and cargo vessels assaulted, outlying settlements overrun, even a town or two. Like here, it was a one-sided fight with the living on the losing side. Until these skeletal armies suddenly started screaming and retreating. All reports say it was about the time you blew the Horn of the Gods." Blackthorne paused, before adding, "Apparently that thing has quite the range."

"How much damage? Casualties?"

"Could have been worse. Men and women were lost, and vessels were battered. Nothing sunk, though. The worst was Evermarsh. Most of that settlement is in ruins. Its people vanished. No one knows if they were killed and taken or if they escaped. Not yet, at least."

Rafe felt like he had been punched in the gut. He remembered Evermarsh as a quaint settlement between Llansfoot and Pentown, nestled in a beautiful cove. Each summer they held a fire festival and a trade market.

"There's something else, Captain." Blackthorne's voice cut through his thoughts. "We've been called to sail to Crickwell Town. The Navy's sending more ships here and have asked us to join a council they've convened."

Rafe scowled. "We haven't the time to divert to Crickwell Town. It's even more important than ever we get to Rock Island."

"Yes, sir, but I think we should make time." Blackthorne swallowed noticeably and fidgeted. "Apparently, your sister is coming."

Surprised replaced Rafe's annoyance. "My...which one?"

"The Goddess of the Sea."

"Lynna?" Rafe's mouth curled into a grin despite the circumstances. "Lynna's going to a Navy council? I can imagine the entrance she'll make." The captain chuckled and then composed himself. "But you're right, we will have to go. If she's leaving the sea, something is seriously wrong. We need to find out what."

"Yes, sir. My thinking as well. In addition, Lord Merrill's waiting there, and they asked us to bring Pelham." Blackthorne glanced over at the moaning man. "Is he good to travel? Will he come?"

"I think so. We'll take the body of his officer, Lieutenant Commander Montague with us. He wants to see to the burial, and he'll most likely go where it goes."

Blackthorne sighed. "Never thought I'd feel sorry for the man, but I never thought I'd see this either. At least Montague's family will have a burial. There's not another body to be found, and reports from the survivors say men, living and dead, were dragged into the sea. I shudder to think of their fate."

"I think we both know. They belong to Ashetus now." Rafe clenched his fingers into a fist. "But we'll set them free." He looked around at the ruin of the *Sea's Favour*. "We'll set the whole of the worlds free."

When the *Celestial Jewel* sailed into Crickwell Town harbour, a company of naval ships crowded the docking berths, and none of the usual rowdy bluster rang out to greet them.

Rafe watched them drift in to dock from the main deck also keeping an eye on Pelham. The commander refused to leave Montague's body, which had been laid out on deck for the trip. His remains had been carefully shrouded and strewn with strong smelling herbs and wrapped in a canvas tarp provided by the Navy of the Royal Court. Throughout the short voyage, Pelham never said a word.

They manoeuvred into port, and the harbour crews worked in silence to get the *Jewel* settled in her mooring, successfully anchoring her in a safe berth. Naval officers hailed from the docks moments later.

"Permission to come aboard, Captain Morrow, and escort you and Commander Pelham to the council!"

Despite sudden misgivings, Rafe shouted back. "Permission granted!"

Rafe met the naval officers, a company of three men,

as they boarded. With him, he carried a satchel. "Welcome to my ship, gentlemen. I wish it were under better circumstances."

The ranking officer nodded in greeting. "So do I, sir. I'm Lieutenant Vaughan. If you and Commander Pelham are ready, we should depart. Your sister's been asking for you, and I think it best you show up sooner than later."

"Lynna's already here?" Rafe suppressed a smile. "Then yes, we'd better go." He turned his head slightly. "Pelham. It's time to leave."

The commander looked up. "What about Montague?"

Rafe sighed, but gently replied, "I'm sure one of these officers can see to arrangements." Rafe addressed Vaughan, explaining. "We have the body of Lieutenant Commander Francis Montague on board. Can you leave one of your men to make arrangements to have the body transferred to naval custody?"

"A body?" The words seem to shock the lieutenant. "You have a body?" Then he recovered his composure. "Of course, the Navy of the Royal Court takes care of its own." He turned to the midshipman on his right. "See to it, Boyd."

The pale midshipman nodded, scurried over to Pelham, and exchanged a few words. Moments later, the commander joined Rafe and the two other naval officers.

He squared his shoulders and straightened his spine addressing everyone. "I'm ready, gentlemen. Sorry for the delay."

Lieutenant Vaughan nodded and gave a quick salute. "Understandable, sir." Both he and his remaining man turned to leave. "Shall we? Everyone's eager to have you join them."

Rafe tucked his satchel under his arm, stepped on to the gangplank, and the group walked down to the dock. Lieutenant Vaughan then escorted them to the Guild Hall where the council awaited them.

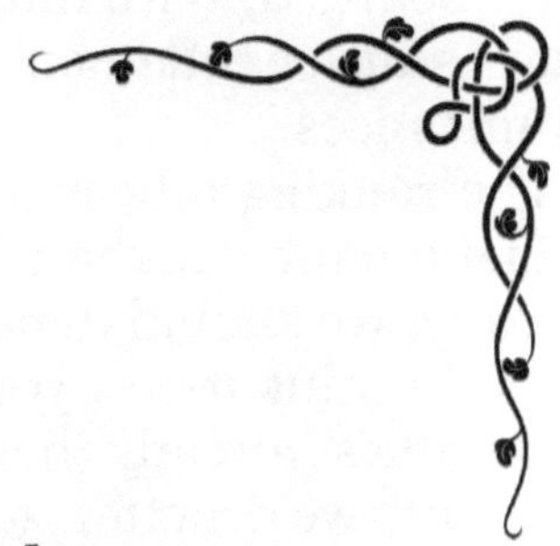

Chapter Eighteen

Council of War

Rafe walked inside the Guild Hall vestibule to the sounds of arguing voices, his sister's mocking laughter and Lord Merrill shouting for order. With a sigh, he marched into the main hall, Pelham and Lieutenant Vaughan following.

He stopped a few feet into the room restraining the simultaneous urges to laugh and turn tail. Clusters of naval officers scattered around the hall engaged in debate with Lord Merrill the only one at the council table vainly calling for order. His sister Lynna, dressed thankfully in a long coat, had perched herself on top of a sturdy cabinet where she dripped seawater and flicked droplets at the head of a Navy captain. The captain, in turn, appeared to be lecturing her on decorum and a proper dress code while ogling the lower half of her bare legs.

Rafe took a breath ready to put an end to the madness, but Pelham beat him to it.

"This is disgraceful!" The commander's shout boomed out across the room with the force of a hurricane drawing everyone's attention. "We're here to defeat an enemy, not bicker like children! Do your duty men! We are naval officers!" He brushed past Rafe and strode to the table where he sat beside an astonished Lord Merrill. Pelham folded his arms and glared out at the assembly.

Lynna broke the sudden silence. "Brother! Finally! These humans are so tedious. I don't know how you stand them." She jumped down from her perch, startling the naval captain. She turned her gaze to Pelham. "Except perhaps that one. He seems to have some sense at least, and that Lord of yours...He's amusing." She walked to the council table and settled into a chair beside Pelham giving him a smile. "Come, brother. Sit down so we can get this over with."

Rafe crossed the room and took a seat opposite the trio. He placed his satchel on the table. The rest of the naval officers sat down in available chairs.

"So, why am I here?"

"Because we need someone to figure out a way to mount a defence against these—these skeleton soldiers." Lord Merrill smacked the table in frustration and anger. "Before their next strike." He turned to Lynna. "Tell him, Miss Lynna."

Rafe quirked an eyebrow and a corner of his mouth at his sister being referred to as 'miss' but turned his attention to her as she spoke.

"They're gathered under the sea, brother. An army. Hundreds of corpses and skeletons, all around the islands. I cannot move down there anymore without seeing them." She shivered and then anger flashed in her eyes. "They've taken over my home! I won't stand for it!" She suddenly leaned forward, water trickling across the table. "They mean to take over this one as well. I heard their whispers and their cries. The whole sea is screaming with their voices. I cannot take it anymore! They have to go before they infest everything!" She gave a frustrated cry and slammed against the back of her chair rocking it slightly.

"I may be able to help with that." Rafe opened the satchel and withdrew the horn. "I found the Horn of the Gods." Lord Merrill gave an undignified whoop, but Lynna gave him a quizzical look. He added, "Ulerne's hunting horn."

Her eyes widened, and she gasped. "But—but…I thought that was just a story Father wove to amuse us."

"He told you of this?" Rafe frowned.

"Yes, when I was young. He used to tell me stories to help me sleep. Didn't he tell you these tales?"

Rafe shook his head, tucking away his puzzlement for another day. "Another one of his secrets, I suppose. In any case, I used it against our skeleton hordes. It drove off the creatures attacking Commander Pelham's ship and may have done the same to the other invading swarms."

Lynna smiled. "That explains why those nasty creatures suddenly returned to the sea en masse screaming as if the Kraken chased them." Then she frowned. "But it only worked above the sea. The dead below in the water didn't react. Not until the others came back. Then they shook and moaned like a thousand broken rattles. I had to come to the surface to finish the journey to this quaint little place."

"Interesting. It does seem to have limits." Rafe ran a finger along the edge of the horn.

"Perhaps." Lynna spoke softly as if contemplating something. "Perhaps it only works in one place at a time. Above or below."

"What are you thinking, sister?"

"I don't know. Just bits of old stories running through my head." She smiled enigmatically. "May I see it?"

"Of course." Rafe picked up the horn and handed it to his sister.

She held it gingerly with both hands, her tapered fingers curling around the bell end. "It's warm like the currents around the Stone Fire Islands." She trembled and tilted her head. "I can feel its magic. It almost feels alive. It tingles under my fingers and tastes of summer lightning."

Rafe leaned forward. "You can feel that? I could sense something, but not the sensations you describe."

"Yes, I can feel it. Like a fierce storm and a calm sea, like the midday sun and the stars at night all swirling together. It's fascinating. It's intoxicating." She stared for a minute and abruptly handed it to Rafe. "Here. Take it back." She folded her arms and sighed. Rafe stowed the horn into the confines of the satchel.

"This is all very enlightening, but we still need a plan." Lord Merrill broke into the conversation. "I've ordered all surviving ships, naval and cargo, into the closest ports to fortify our defences. Assembled here at the council, are naval captains and other officers from Abersythe, Crickwell Island, Llansfoot, and Storm Point. We need to formulate a strategy and relay it across the Navy of the Royal Court. We've already lost a third of the Black Shoals fleet with sailors gone and damaged ships. Tenby has lost ships as well as Pentown. Another concentrated attack could cripple the Navy."

"A sound move, bringing the ships into shore. They're far more vulnerable on the open sea than in port. I think we—"

Whatever Rafe would have said went unspoken as a frantic midshipman burst into the room, screaming. "A wave is heading this way! Bones! Masses of bones! We're under attack!"

Rafe leapt to his feet, seeing Pelham turn pale and Lynna snarl. She scrambled over the table and raced across the hall as he grabbed the horn and chased her outside.

Lynna raced through the streets to the docks, straight to the edge of the water. A shadow smeared across the horizon as a giant shrieking wave barrelled inland. Lynna roared in defiance spreading her arms wide, a burst of pale green light flaring from her body. Beyond the harbour, another wave rose, the sea ascending in colours of emerald and cerulean, an outward tide rushing to meet the legions of Ashetus. The two walls of ocean crashed together in a scream of spray and cracking bone, Lynna's force of magic and will hammering the opposite swell of sea and horror deep below the surface.

Rafe joined her side as the last of the water fell back into the sea. "Nicely done."

"It won't hold them for long. They'll regroup or more creatures will arrive. They'll attack again soon, probably within the hour."

"You've done this before?"

She nodded. "At Shadow Cay. They attacked three times before giving up or moving on to another target."

"Your temple is on Shadow Cay."

"Yes. They didn't touch it. I didn't let them."

A scuffling of feet and whispers made the pair turn. Several naval officers and sailors stood behind them all staring at Lynna, looks of awe on their faces. Beyond her ring of admirers, Rafe saw Lord Merrill, Pelham, and the naval men from the council.

"That was marvellous, ma'am! Simply marvellous!" A lieutenant commander blurted out his enthusiasm for Lynna's quick action.

She glared. "It was nothing. And temporary. Make yourselves useful and man some defences for the port. They'll be back and we must be ready."

Surprisingly, every man snapped to attention as if awaiting her next order, and she gave it. "I want a line of armed men along the docks and patrols along the shoreline outside the town. If this place has cannons, I want them primed, manned, and pointed out to sea."

In minutes, the naval officers, sailors, and the captains from the council raced to carry out her commands. Only Lord Merrill and Pelham remained on the docks with Rafe and Lynna.

They walked forward, Lord Merrill chuckling. "It

seems the skill of command runs in your family."

"Indeed." Pelham added his voice. "And with your permission, ma'am, I'll join the defence crews. I've battled these things up close, and I believe I can provide useful instruction for combat if any manage to slip past the two of you." Pelham nodded at Rafe and Lynna.

"Permission granted, Commander." Lynna smiled at him, and Pelham blushed before hurrying off.

Lord Merrill remained for a moment. "I should see to things as well, but, may I ask, what are your plans to hold these attacks at bay?"

"I'll take the *Jewel* out into the harbour. It should afford a better position to use the horn." Rafe noticed Lynna glance at the instrument in his hand before speaking.

"Yes, that will give you a better vantage point. I'll return to the sea. I can see more, do more, from the water." She tossed her head, shucked off her coat, and jumped into the harbour.

Lord Merrill gaped as she left, but quickly drew together his composure. "She's not one for modesty, is she?"

Rafe shook his head, hiding his amusement. "But she is powerful, and that's what we need at the moment."

"Undeniably." Lord Merrill extended his hand, and Rafe shook it gladly. "Good luck, Captain. I fear we will need it to survive this all."

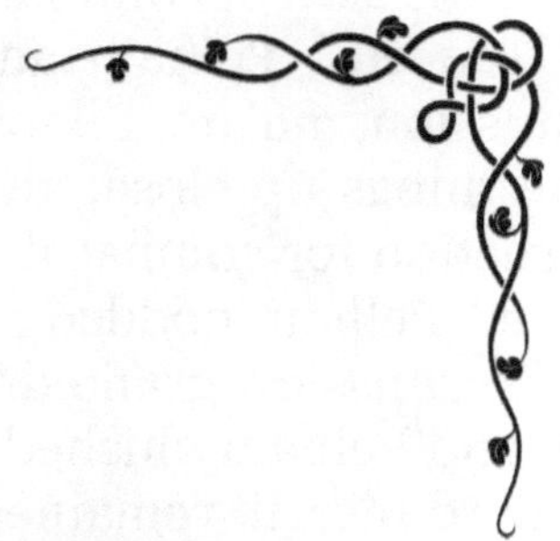

Chapter Nineteen

Battles

Rafe stood on the quarterdeck of his ship, Blackthorne at his side. They had sailed from their berth to the middle of Crickwell harbour in record time with the help of a diligent dock crew, Lynna, and a little magic.

"Are we going to make it through this time, Captain?"

"I think so. Between myself and Lynna, we should be able to drive them back and away from Crickwell Town."

"I don't mean here, sir. I saw what that horn did at the bay and what your sister did in this very harbour. I'm sure we can hold off their attacks here. I mean the whole of it. We haven't retrieved the Bow yet, and we're not even on our way there. And with these attacks on the islands, we're needed here with the horn. It feels like we're being deliberately delayed as if Ashetus was playing a waiting game, running out our time."

"I know it does, and that may well be what's happening. I have some thoughts on the matter, my friend, and a possible solution to our dilemma." He patted a sack that he had slung over his shoulder, a bag that held the horn, traded for the more cumbersome satchel. "Lynna said there are hundreds of Ashetus' hordes under the sea, yet, so far, only scattered companies of these soldiers have surfaced."

"Hundreds?" Blackthorne's voice trembled a touch. "Why haven't they invaded then? Testing our defences possibly?"

"Possibly. Or Ashetus isn't powerful enough yet to control them all at once. Either way, I think we may be fighting them on the wrong side of the ocean."

"The wrong side?" Bewilderment chased the first mate's words.

"Yes. We used the horn from the ship above the sea's surface. Our enemy is underneath the water."

"Under—oh!" A look of comprehension blossomed on Blackthorne's face. "You mean Lynna. You want her to use it. Do you think she can?"

Rafe nodded. "She examined it at the council. It responded to her or she to it. On a deeper level than I did. I think it is meant for her, not me."

"Then," Blackthorne paused, his mouth frowning, "why keep it? Shouldn't she have it to use in this battle?"

"For this battle, I doubt it will make a difference which of us uses it as the creatures must surface. I want to get an idea of its power before I give it to her. The taste I got at the bay suggests it holds immense magic. If she can tap into it more than I, she could unleash a very destructive force. If that's the case, her using it around a settlement may not be a good idea."

"I see the sense in that. No point courting more trouble."

"No. We get through this and then pass it on to her. Then we retrieve the bow." Rafe laid a hand on the rail. "And to answer your original question, we will get through this. We've survived it so far, we'll make it to the end." He stared out at the sea. "We won't lose, Blackthorne. We can't lose."

The second wave came from the west, larger than the first, but still full of shrieking tormented dead, jangling their bones and gesticulating decayed flesh. Cries of 'Attack!' echoed from the dock, and, from the sea outside the harbour, Lynna rose up on a mighty wave screaming a frenzied battle cry. She conjured more waves in front of her and sent them careening forward smashing into the new assault force. In an instant, the skeletal wave dissipated, the dead dropping into the sea, and Lynna's waves met empty air.

Rafe watched it all from the deck of his ship, waiting.

When Ashetus' soldiers rose again in another wall of seawater, this time behind Lynna, he blew the horn. It howled, loud and rough, a golden ripple shaking across the air between the ship and the breaker full of the dead. Their tormented voices screamed and faltered, and some of the dead fell back into the sea. The majority of their attack broke off into a series of smaller, multiple forces, closer to the surface but still surging towards the town.

Rafe sounded the horn again and again while Lynna pounded them with counter waves from behind until their defence drowned the enemy wails under the surface. For a moment, peace reigned. But only for a moment.

Another cry of 'Attack!' followed by 'Man the cannon!' resounding from the town filled the silence. Rafe scanned the water but found no sign of wave or bone. He turned to see a legion of skeletons storming across the beaches, over the crags, past the edge of town. The boom of cannon sounded, and explosions burst across the beach in fractured clouds of sand and bone splinters. Another boom of cannon and more skeletal soldiers fell, yet, still, the legions of the dead advanced, flooding to the edges of town. Naval officers rushed to engage the enemy, and, as Rafe put the horn to his lips, he saw Pelham leading the charge.

The captain sounded the horn, a screaming shriek of noise, a wail challenging the dead to dare defy him. The army of Ashetus answered the blast of the horn with a howl of their own, many falling or thrashing about. Pelham and his officers waded into the fray, slashing and hacking as Rafe smashed another blast of the horn into the air. The second horde of attackers retreated, chased to the water by the Navy.

Lynna swam out, diving down deep. She surfaced with the shout of, 'They're retreating!' before diving under again. Rafe relaxed a fraction as he watched the Navy regroup and his sister patrol the waters just outside the harbour. He turned as he heard a noise behind him to see Blackthorne scanning the beach and town with a spyglass.

"What do you see?"

"The beach and the dunes are torn up from the cannon fire, but I'm not seeing Navy casualties or the enemy. I think we won this round, sir."

"And hopefully bought a reprieve. The ship stays here for a bit to mind things in case they return. I'm going to have a chat with my sister." Adjusting the strap on his shoulder, he slipped the horn back in its sack and summoned his magic. He floated over the rail and across the harbour to keep pace with his sister as she swam.

"Why are you here? We've driven them off for now. No need to search. I can handle it, and it's unlikely they'll come back now. That horn of yours hurts them too much."

"I know. The Horn is why I've come. I think you're the one who should be wielding it."

She stopped swimming, turning to face him. She bobbed on the surface her expression wide-eyed and shocked. "Me? But—but why?" Her voice held disbelief, yet her eyes stared at the bag slung over his shoulder.

"This instrument responded to you far more than me, and, while I can use it, I can only do so on land or on board my ship. You may be able to use this under the sea."

"Under the—" She grinned. "That's your plan?"

"It is. Will you try?"

She nodded. "Yes. I'll try."

As soon as it became safe, the *Jewel* left Crickwell Town with Lynna on board and sailed in haste to the seas past Razor Reef and on to Rock Island. When safely in an open expanse of water, Rafe ordered a heave to and the dropping of the ship's sea anchor. As the ship slowed, Rafe joined his sister at the stern—the horn tucked under his arm—where she gazed at her ocean, at her domain.

"Are you certain I can do this? That horn—"

"Is powerful, I know. But you're more than a match for it."

She snorted. "We'll see." She held out her hand. "Give me the thing before I change my mind."

Rafe placed the Horn of the Gods in her outstretched palm. He watched her inhale a breath and let it out slowly. "I can feel it. So fierce, so eager. It wants the fight, brother." She curled her fingers around the horn's neck and claimed possession. Then she climbed on to the ship's rail, her teal-coloured hair fluttering in the wind. "Time to test the whole of it, brother."

She leapt from the rail in a graceful, backward dive. With a flick of her wrist, the sea came up to meet her, wrapping her body in a swell of water, pulling her under and away from the wake and rudder of the *Jewel*.

Rafe leaned over the railing and watched her surface, her hand raised, waving the horn. She put the instrument to her lips hesitating for a fraction of a moment. Then she drew a breath, sank beneath the sea, and blew a note from the Horn of the Gods.

The muffled, congruous sound came bursting out like wild horses ripping through the water in a wild ride. The ocean bucked recklessly, rocking the ship, and shuddered a vibration through the *Jewel's* bones. Pale emerald mist swirled in its wake settling on top of the water like foam. Just under the surface, Lynna lowered the horn from her mouth and clutched it to her chest. Then she surfaced.

Rafe shouted down to her. "Well, it seems as if you can use it! How do you feel?"

She turned her head upward, a laughing smile lighting up her face. "Magnificent! I can do this brother! I can do this! And I know just where to start. There was a small band submerged by the West Shoal Reef. A perfect place to try it out on them." She stared at Rafe, waiting.

He nodded, adding, "We'll head to Rock Island and then back to Shadow Cay to meet at your shrine! Keep safe, sister!"

"I will!" She shouted a farewell, holding the horn above her head like a prize. Then she disappeared beneath the waves.

✳

The *Celestial Jewel* left Lynna to her work and sailed full speed to Rock Island, storming into the Blue Bay harbour as soon as the ship was able. Two naval vessels and armed sailors with salutes and grim faces greeted them as they docked in port. Even here, they could see signs of fighting and invasion, and the captain wondered how they held off the skeleton hordes. After docking, Rafe gave Blackthorne orders to hold the ship and disembarked alone. He eschewed a solitary walk, instead using his magic to propel him to the temple in the quickest way possible.

He descended at its gates, enshrouded in a misty cloud of blue, to find the entrance open to him. He strode in through the garden and was met by Rayla near the temple's main doors. Oddly, she held a lit lantern although it was daylight.

"The Oracle said to expect you and escort you to the

old underground passageways." She bowed slightly. "She said we should leave immediately, so if you will come this way."

She walked off without another word, and Rafe followed her, though he knew the way without her assistance. If the Oracle wanted her to accompany him, it would be important.

The duo meandered their way through the garden and out a side gate to the area behind the temple. They passed the pergola and the temple's well coming to what appeared to be an abandoned stone outbuilding.

"We're here." Rayla broke the silence that had settled between them and opened the door to the building. She held up the lantern, illuminating a stairwell carved from the rock, leading underground. She started down the steps, lighting their path as Rafe followed. He pulled the door almost shut behind them, leaving it open just a crack.

They descended the narrow, winding staircase to an underground alcove with another door. Rayla produced a key from her pocket and handed it to Rafe.

"You may do the honours. This opens into the tunnels, as you know. The Oracle told me to take you to the old Oracle Chamber. She said that's where you need to be."

This surprised Rafe. Though he had traversed the tunnels before, he had never ventured into that sacred space out of respect for his priestesses. It spoke of secrets in his own house, and he filed away that bit of information to be discussed at a later date.

But to Rayla, he said nothing but merely turned the key in the lock, and heard it release with a click.

Chapter Twenty

Waves and Shadows

A world away, Lynna swam the outer rim of West Shoals Reef, the horn grasped tightly in her hand. A group of skeletons, newly rotting corpses, and bodies of various states of decay in-between milled along the spread of coral and rock, wailing and scraping their bones. She circled around the mass repeatedly, studying every inch of the battleground and the number of her enemy.

She eventually chose her place and swam to just off-centre of the mid-point of the reef. Yet she lingered there on the edge of the gathered dead, hesitating to use the horn. The truth bubbled up in her thoughts, the truth she didn't confide in her brother. That under the anger and the outrage she felt fear. Fear of the darkness contaminating her seas, a fright that echoed the dread felt by her creatures. She was scared of those abhorrent things before her and was terrified of their master: the beast, the abomination that plucked the dead from their rest. She shuddered to think such a monster existed, could breathe twisted life into sea-buried bones, and it made her want to flee. But what terrified her most of all lay in her hand.

The Horn of the Gods.

The power she sensed, the connection she felt, intoxicated her, nearly overwhelmed her in its fierce beauty and light. It called to her, called to be used, to spread its majesty over the sea and purge the darkness. To purge it everywhere: sea, land, beyond into the realm of the gods. To bend everything to the light, everything to her will. And in the darkest corners of her heart, the thought appealed to her. That's what frightened her. Her willingness to give in to the Horn and change the world. She hesitated to use that power lest she succumb.

Yet, what choice do I have?

She closed her eyes and let the rhythm of the sea surround her, the pressure of the ocean, the taste of it, the echo infused into her magic. She let herself drown in it until they were one. She let her power apex, her mind awash in conflict, but allowed it flow, determined to take up the battle.

The sea is mine, you remnants, you bits of animated bones. Now I show you why.

She inhaled, her lungs expanding with air, with sea, with energy. She raised the Horn and felt a tingle along her skin. She sensed the wash of tide and current, the taste of brine, and the scent of a storm on the air. She felt her power, the raw might of the sea, build and swell, and wisps of green flowed along her skin and hair. She placed her lips on the warm mouthpiece of the horn and blew a hurricane of both breath and magic into the Horn of the Gods.

A crystal clear note of song burst out; a clarity of power singing life, verve, and light into the sea. A wave rumbled forth, a surge of something ancient, something past infinity. A power beyond the small spark of mortality, past even death.

It moved like a tsunami through the water, like an unstoppable tide rushing towards destruction. Every dead eye and hollowed bone socket turned to face it, screaming an unhallowed wail of wretched misery and salvation. In that moment, Lynna knew the dead welcomed their own annihilation.

The shockwave from the Horn hit them dead on, crushing bones against the reef in cracks and pops and splinters. Rotting flesh dissolved or sliced away, goo and chum washed away for the fishes. Within minutes, the horde of undead became a pile of bones and decayed flesh.

And not one corpse moved or twitched or rose again from their final resting place.

Lynna smiled. She felt a peace. A purpose. Satisfaction and exhilaration coursed through her blood, momentarily erasing her fears. She patted the Horn.

We have much work to do, you and I.

An echo of the Horn rose to the sky to be met with dark laughter. The Nightmare Crow flew among the clouds, a malicious glee chasing his wings. "See, Ashetus, see! It begins! It begins!" The Crow dove, a spinning black streak descending from the sky to the sea, pulling up before striking to glide over the ocean's surface. "They are coming for you! Soon you will be mine!"

He skimmed the tip of a wing on the sea and screeched a cry of triumph and rage, reaching far, far beyond the mortal world to the ears of an ancient being...

Below the worlds, Ashetus gnashed its teeth, and frenzy fuelled the hot red glow in its eyes. Its tentacles lashed, its body smashed bones, and it dreamed of bloodied feathers and a broken Horn.

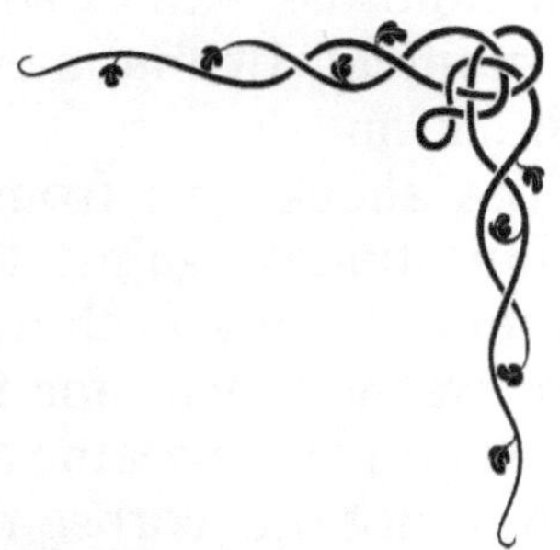

Chapter Twenty-One

The Hunter's Bow

As the lock on the tunnel entrance clicked, Rafe pushed open the alcove's stone door revealing a long dark passage. Rayla held up her lantern letting the light illuminate the ancient corridor. It revealed cobwebs, dust, and grimy stone. Stale air wafted out with the faint stench of mould.

Rayla wrinkled her nose. "No ghosts or monsters, but I could do without the smell."

Rafe smiled. "This is nothing. Once, I was locked in a ship's hold with a barrel of rotting fish and men that hadn't washed for weeks."

The corner of her mouth quirked. "The hazards of life at sea?"

"Something like that." He smiled. "But it's not important. Shall we?" Rafe walked into the passageway, Rayla a step behind him.

As their feet trod on dirt and natural rock, Rafe ran his fingers over the wall construction. "The tunnel walls are quality masonry. I never noticed before, but I think it's older than the temple. I'd wager another structure was repaired and integrated into the temple's foundation.

I always thought these passages were created with the temple. I wonder what they were originally?"

"Amaratha," Rayla's voice caught for a moment on the name. "Came down here some years ago before she closed them off and studied their design. She thought they might have been part of a shrine to some older deity. She found odd symbols and markings, but never found a match to them."

"A mystery for another day, I hope." He sighed. "How far to the old Oracle's Chamber?"

"Only a few minutes. The passage branches off soon, and we go right. The chamber is just beyond that."

They walked the rest of the distance in silence, stirring grime and cool, damp, musty air until they arrived at the underground chamber.

"Here it is, the Chamber of the Oracle." Rayla reached out, turned the handle of the mouldering wooden door, and pushed it open. It creaked on worn and rusty hinges. "Not much to look at anymore."

The pair stepped past the doorway, and Rafe scanned the room. A cramped square space with only a dusty, half-broken chair within its walls.

"Sad, seeing it like this." Rayla murmured, her voice tinged in regret. "Some of the old writings in the library have illustrations of this place. It was beautiful. Painted walls were lit with candles. Now it sits in the dark with the paint worn off from age." She sighed. "That chair used to be red velvet and gilt with an altar behind it."

"An altar?" Rayla nodded at Rafe's question. "Take the light closer. I want to examine the wall."

They stepped across the room and Rafe peered at the wall behind the chair. He noticed rough lines etched into the stone, and ran his fingers over the indentations.

"I think this is what we're searching for. That feels like a Sign of the Star to me."

"Now what? I see no bow or box or anything to indicate

a treasure."

"Now we look for a hiding place. Tear this room apart if we have to." Rafe laid a hand over the symbol etched in the stone and pressed. Nothing budged. "There must be some indication. Perhaps it's underneath or opposite or—"

"Above. Stars are above."

"What?" Rafe instinctively looked up but saw nothing but a stone ceiling.

"Not here. In the sky. In the night sky. They are light. Perhaps this one needs light." She momentarily laid her hand over Rafe's. "Give it light, Exalted One, and see what happens."

Rafe looked at her a moment pondering the quickness of her answer before replying. "It is a thought, that. Wait outside. If something happens it may be safer."

She nodded, moving away until only a faint glimmer of light shone through the doorway. Rafe stood alone in the dark and took a breath. Then he danced a sliver of his magic through the lines in the stone, breathing radiance into the Sign of the Star. When he took his hand away, the stone still pulsed blue.

A faint hum began then louder, growing in volume until it filled the room. The light on the wall fluttered a rhythm to match the hum, growing ever brighter with each beat. The ground under his feet rumbled and, suddenly, the light, the star, and the wall burst outward in a spray of pulverized debris and dust. Rafe twisted away from the explosion, shielding his face.

"Are you all right?" Rayla dashed back into the room, which flooded in the glow of her lantern.

"I'm fine. Just covered in filth, and—" he stopped speaking, staring at the gaping hole in the wall and the rectangular alcove beyond. There, hanging on a hook, was a bow.

"Well," Rayla sniffed. "I thought that would be more difficult. And less volatile." She crossed the room and shone her lantern next to the hidden recess.

"Don't touch it!" Rafe shouted and moved to stop her if she reached inside the niche.

"Wasn't planning on it. I'm not stupid." She glared. "I just want a look at the thing." She lifted her lantern higher, studying the weapon. "It's not wood. I'm not certain what material it's made from. And it appears unblemished. No age, no dust, no wear. If this is as old as you say, that's amazing."

"Not if it was forged by magic. By gods. But you're right, that's not wood. It looks like the same material as the Horn. Something beyond our world, I think."

"Fascinating, but it's time to take your prize, I believe."

"Yes. I suppose it is. Stand back." Rayla retreated a few steps and Rafe reached into the nook. The moment he wrapped his fingers around the bow, he felt its power, an energy, unlike anything he had experienced. He knew in that moment that they all stood a chance against Ashetus.

He plucked the bow off its hook with a held breath and withdrew the weapon. Nothing happened, and he exhaled. "Let's get out of here, back to the temple."

Rayla nodded. They hurried back through the passageways and ascended to the temple proper. Rafe dusted off his coat, shaking the stone debris from his hair, and gave Rayla a nod farewell.

"I hate to cut my visit short, but I have to—"

"Not yet." Rayla snapped the words, surprising Rafe into silence. "You have someone waiting to see you first. She says she has something for you, a gift."

Gift. The word caught all of Rafe's attention as the Grey Sisters' voices echoed in his head. "Where?"

"Follow me."

Rayla led him through the temple halls and left him standing in front of a closed door. Rafe turned the handle and entered the room. Bevire sat in a chair by a window holding something wrapped in cloth on her lap. Rafe paused mid-stride and stared before slowly walking to her side.

"Hello, brother." She didn't turn her head as she traced patterns on the window glass with her fingers. "It is more beautiful than I expected. This world of yours. All this light and colour. Not as comforting as mine, though. And not as peaceful as the Isle of Shadows. Too many sharp edges and nowhere to hide. Not anymore." She turned at last to face her brother.

"Why are you here? Did Father send you?"

She smiled. "Oh no. What he knows of me these days is a mystery. I pray he knows nothing, but I suspect he may know everything. More than we two, even. Father keeps his secrets when it pleases him and shares them when it's useful."

"Why are you here?" Rafe repeated the question, fearing the answer.

"To confess. To make amends. To beg forgiveness." She sighed. "I listened to dark words and let fear direct my actions. I should have ignored the Crow, ignored the world perhaps, and let you be." She let out a breath and stroked the edge of the cloth in her lap. "You have always frightened me, brother, and I let that fear rule me. I told myself you were dangerous, that it was what needed to be done. I let the Crow's lies, his deceit, convince me though I knew I shouldn't."

Foreboding skipped along Rafe's skin, dancing with shivers. "What did you do, sister?"

She stared, a film of tears welling in her eyes. "I am the one that broke the seal. I let Ashetus out of his prison. To try and use him against you."

A feeling of betrayal broke across Rafe's thoughts, surprising him. There was never a closeness between them, but his heart still broke that she would do this, move against him in this manner. She never spoke the words, but he knew she meant his destruction as a result of her actions.

When he felt able to control his words, he spoke. "I did not know you hated me that much. That you would risk the worlds to see me...gone." He could not say it aloud. Dead. She wanted him dead.

"No." She looked at him, her eyes full of tears and sorrow. "I did not risk that. I did not know what I raised." She lowered her gaze. "But that is no excuse for I did not ask either. I chose to ignore my good sense. To ignore the misgivings I felt." She sighed. "But know this. I do not, I never will, hate you. I—I am afraid of you. In some ways you...you favour Mother too much." She sighed. "And I walk in the dark. I know what lives there. What you can control if you wanted. That possibility terrifies me."

A small inkling of understanding crept into his thoughts with a pang of sympathy. "I am not her, Bevire. I will never be her. And what I am is not my doing. Despite all of your opinions. Why do you think I accepted exile so long ago? I know how my family feels. I've always known. I never held it against you even if I wished it different."

His sister glanced up again, surprise mingling with her tears. She replied, disbelief in her tone. "But you and Father, always so angry. So bitter. I thought you hated us all. Resented us."

"No. Like you, I don't hate my family. But some of Father's actions...you of all of us know how he is, his secrets, his lies. That is what comes between us...causes the quarrels."

"I'm sorry. I shouldn't have interfered. I shouldn't have worked the Crow's spell."

"You aren't the first to fall for his tricks." Rafe let a sigh escape his lips, and then a half-smile. "Help me now to right your mistake."

She matched his smile. "That I have already done. The other reason I came. To make amends." She unfolded the cloth and held up the arrow. "For your new bow." She nodded at the weapon he still held. "I plucked a feather from that wretched crow and fashioned this arrow from it. From that and darkness itself, binding it in name magic. This will kill Ashetus if your aim is true with that weapon."

Rafe held out his hand. Bevire placed the arrow in his hand and sighed a soft sound of relief. He curled his fingers around the projectile: the arrow in one hand, the bow in the other.

"Thank you, sister."

She sighed again, but with a smile on her face.

Rafe turned to go. He walked a few steps and stopped, twisted around to look at his sister. "Come with me. Sail with me to fight Ashetus."

"What?" A mix of disbelief and fear shadowed her face. "Why would you want me?"

Rafe hesitated, unsure how to put what he was feeling into words. Finally, he said, "The Grey Sisters told me I needed to bring an army. I prefer family." He gathered the arrow and the bow in one hand and held the other out to Bevire. "Come with me."

She slowly rose, walking towards Rafe. She tentatively reached out her hand until she, at last, grasped her brother's. They smiled at each other and left the temple together.

"This is marvellous!" Bevire stood at the rail of his ship, laughing, the wind blowing her dark hair. "I can taste salt in the air!" She licked her lips with another laugh. "Your mortal world is most strange. Small things scattered together, weaving patterns and the breath of wonder into substance. Most strange, but marvellous."

Rafe looked on in amusement, remarking, "I'm glad you're enjoying the voyage."

"I am. This vessel is delightful." Then her face clouded for a moment. "I just wish the reasons that brought me here were as pleasant."

Rafe moved to her side. "Time enough for worry later. Sometimes you simply have to enjoy the day."

She smiled at him, and they both stared out at the passing sea and the sky as the *Celestial Jewel* raced its way to Shadow Cay.

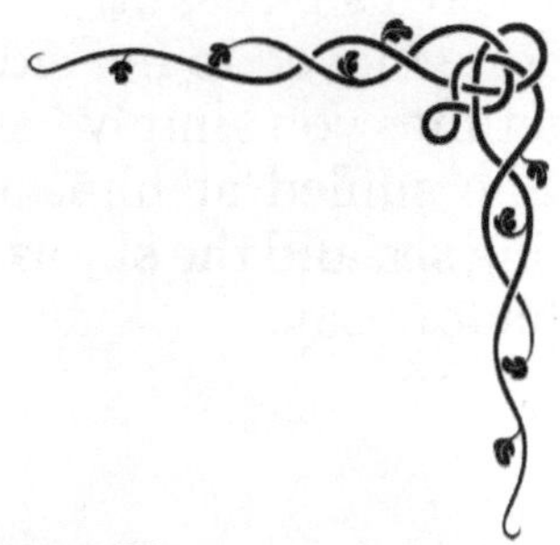

Chapter Twenty-Two

A Victory

The *Celestial Jewel* sailed towards the Bay of the Moon off the Shadow Cay coast in sight of Lynna's temple shrine. Rafe and Bevire stood on deck when a shout rang across the ship.

"Waterspout! Off the starboard side!"

A great fountain of seawater erupted from the depths, Lynna riding the spray towards the ship. Her voice rang out, "They're mobilizing! The remainder of the army of the dead are gathering together for an invasion!" The waterspout dissolved, and Lynna dropped gracefully onto the deck. The Horn of the Gods hung from her shoulder, suspended on a cord fashioned of seaweed. "They're headed towards Crickwell Island!"

Rafe raced over to her. "What happened?"

"I wasn't quick enough to get them all in time." A look of anger and disgust crossed her face. "The Horn worked as we hoped, and I swept through Tenby Key, Red Reef, Deep Sea Key, the Stone Fire Islands, and Shadow Cay. The forces there were decimated, but my sea creatures sent me word. The bone legions around Storm Point,

Abersythe, Llansfoot, and the Black Shoals area are on the move. I think the Horn stirred them up. I was on my way to intercept when I saw your ship." She curled her right hand into a fist. "We caught someone's attention, brother."

"Ashetus." Bevire's soft whisper drifted into the conversation.

Lynna glanced at her as if only now aware of her presence. "*You've* come? To join the fight?"

"Yes." Rafe answered for his sister pre-empting any possible confessions. "Bevire brought me an exceptional arrow for the Hunter's Bow. We now have a complete weapon to kill Ashetus."

"Well," Lynna smiled at her sister. "I'm surprised... and glad of it." She turned back to Rafe. "But first we must destroy his rising army."

"Agreed." The captain shouted to his crew, "Full sail! Top speed to Crickwell Island!"

"I can help with that. Get you there faster. As fast as I can swim." Lynna grinned, her eyes sparkling in mischief. "Do you think you can ride one of my waves all the way in?"

Rafe matched her grin, his own eyes dancing. "Try me." He strode to the helm, barking, "I'll take the wheel, Mr. Anders." Anders relinquished the wheel, sliding away with trepidation. Rafe shouted out to the crew, "Hold on to something tight, boys! This will be rough and fast!"

The crew furled out every sail as Lynna leapt over the rail before battening down any loose gear along with themselves. Rafe summoned all his magic and gripped the wheel with both hands, letting his energy flow into the wood. He felt his magic merge with the *Jewel*, the ship snapping power through her keel.

Rafe turned her course heading to Crickwell, a fortunate wind at their back pushing the sails, speed surging them forward. The stern lurched, water crashed against her sides, and the *Jewel's* bow arched upwards as a giant wave swelled underneath the ship and increased the speed threefold.

Sparks of green and blue crackled around the ship, the strength of combined magic accelerating her momentum heaving the ship forward at tremendous speed. Cries and curses echoed from the crew and prayers to every god were sputtered, including the pair of deities that raced them toward Crickwell Island.

They rounded the headland coming into Red Bay in time to see waves of the dead streaming from the swells, attacking the island and the Navy ships defending it. Sea Ghouls shrieked from the air, swooping and diving, harassing ships and the town of Red Bay.

Lynna's wave suddenly dropped, the *Jewel* thumping down on normal tide and a buffer of the ship's magic. The Goddess of the Sea raced away with a cry of, "You're on your own!" outdistancing the *Jewel*.

"Mr. Anders take the wheel!" The sailor grabbed the helm, and Rafe strode across deck shouting, "Blackthorne you have the ship! Take her into the fray, full speed, cannons blazing!" Without breaking stride, he took hold of Bevire's arm pulling her along in his wake. "We need to go, sister. Lynna can handle the attacking dead, but we'll have to deal with the Ghouls."

"Can't you control them?" She struggled in his grip, trying to break free.

"Not anymore. Ashetus rules them now. I need your shadow to help fight them. People will die if we don't help. Time to make amends, Bevire."

She stopped resisting and kept pace, a sudden determined look on her face. "If that's what you need."

The pair summoned their magic in unison and soared from the ship, directly into the battle. They flashed across the sky leaving streaks of black and blue glazing the horizon, tearing into the skies over Red Bay.

A cadre of six ghouls rushed to meet them, their wailing

voices vibrating the air, clawed fingers outstretching to slash. With a snarl of rage and a shout of defiance, Rafe tossed a blast of sizzling blue magic at the nearest of them, shattering their forms into mist. Bevire lashed out with whips of shadow magic, twisting her power around the remaining necks and slicing off their ghostly heads. Severed ghoul remains tumbled into the sea.

More ghouls broke off their attacks on the town and the ships and then swarmed towards the gods. From the sea below them, came the sonorous blast of the Horn of the Gods. The wave of magic-fuelled sound pierced the nub of the invading army, and, in an instant, every creature of the dead shuddered in discordant noise and jarring convulsions. They shrieked a concurrent crescendo of defiled pain, a pinnacle of shouted suffering and fury. Skeletons fell from rigging, collapsed on the beaches, ghouls thrashed and dove into the sea. Above it all, Rafe marvelled at the power unfolding. Lynna harnessed far more of the Horn's might than he had. With those fleeting thoughts, he and Bevire descended.

Another blast from the horn caught the legions of the dead in its grip, smashing breaker and bone, echoing its power across Crickwell Island, and devastating the remaining army. For a moment, there was silence. Then from the depths of the sea came an answering call, a wail of anguish unheard since before the time of mortal men. Such a hideous, primal cry that fear shuddered through blood, bile rose in every throat and brought unbidden tears to the eyes. As the last note of the howl faded, the few invading dead that survived Lynna's final blast fled, racing back far, far below the sea.

Rafe landed on a beach and looked across the water to see Lynna wave the Horn in triumph. He knew this battle was over, if the war still remained to be won. To the west, among the clouds, a black crow flew laughing silently.

The light of the bonfires danced against the night, embers floating skyward to kiss the stars. The rum flowed, and the laughter echoed, the jubilation drifting on the wind. Rafe watched it from a quiet corner of the beach in the lee of a dune, glad of the respite of victory but knowing it was momentary, that the true fight still lay ahead.

Far to his left, singing lustily with a bottle of rum in his hand stood Lieutenant Vaughan surrounded by several equally drunken navy sailors. He saw Lynna swimming offshore, tossing gentle surf back towards Pelham and laughing. He shook his head at the sight, surprised at the odd pairing and their sudden intimate behaviour.

Lynna is always one to take a peculiar liking to people. Quick to size them up. I wonder what she sees in him.

Rafe sighed and let his gaze wander elsewhere. He scanned the crowds for his other sister, not seeing her anywhere.

He murmured under his breath, "Where did you wander off to, Bevire?"

"Right here, brother." Her voice came from the shadows, and Bevire melted out of the dark. "The night on this world is lovely." She looked up at the sky. "The stars have a different glitter here than the Isle of Shadows. Not as bright, but warmer, more mischievous. I think they like your mortals better than the gods."

"Maybe. Maybe the gods hide from them more." Rafe smiled. "But the nights are lovely. One day perhaps I'll show you the view at sea or when our sister's moon is full. It's magnificent."

"I'd like that." She sat down on the sand. "Do you think we'll ever see that time? Do you think we will survive? Or have I doomed this world?" She picked up a handful of sand and let it trickle through her fingers. "I never wanted that. I—I wanted—I don't know what I wanted. Except to stop being afraid." She sighed and smoothed some sand with her palm. "I let my fear rule me. Let the Crow's lies convince me. I was a fool."

Rafe pursed his lips, hesitating. He finally asked the questions crowding his thoughts since the temple. "Why did you fear me so much? What did I do? Are you still afraid?"

"You did nothing. It's nothing you did. It's what you could do." She stared at Rafe, her fingers curling around empty air. "You hold power over each of us, brother, god or mortal. You know that." She turned away, but not before he saw traces of fear flickering in her eyes. "Even gods have souls. Even gods can die at your hands." She turned back before Rafe could reply, her words still tumbling out of her mouth. "So I lived in that shadow, I, Goddess of all Shadows, under yours. That possibility, that fear, ate at me until it nearly consumed me. So I let myself believe the Crow's promises." She hung her head, her next words barely whispered. "The worse thing of all is what I released. I feared the death of gods, yet I released a creature that may be able to kill them, even control them long after death. How pathetically poetic is that fate?"

Rafe smiled soft and with reassurance. "It is not our fate to die. That is the fate of Ashetus. And, listen to me, from someone who has made many blunders in his lifetime, you must learn from your mistakes. Live with your regrets. The past is fixed. You can only change the future." He reached over and laid his hand on her shoulder. "I need you focused on that task, saving our future. With his army driven back, tomorrow we sail to Raven Rock to destroy Ashetus."

Bevire turned her head and smiled. "You are right. The only thing that matters is the death of Ashetus." She turned her head up to stare at the stars. "This ends one way or the other at Raven Rock."

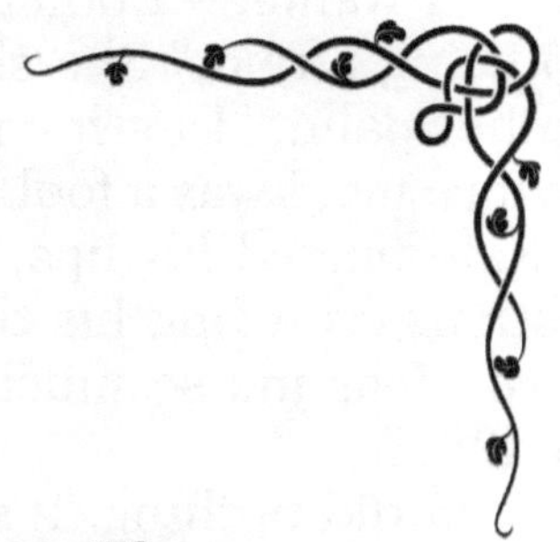

Chapter Twenty-Three

The Summoning

The Grey Sisters stood on the beach to greet them as Rafe, Lynna, and Bevire floated into shore on a wave of their power. The *Celestial Jewel* anchored in the cove's harbour with two naval ships, the *Star's Hope* commanded by Pelham, and the *Sprightly Lark* captained by a newly promoted Commander Vaughan.

The trio of gods landed on the sand, met by cackling laughter.

"Welcome back, God of Souls. You have done well. Driven back the bones, found the bow, and received the gift." The Sisters stared at the bow and makeshift quiver containing Bevire's arrow as well as other arrows slung over Rafe's shoulder. "The black arrow will give a killing shot if you take care to pierce one of its eyes." They stared as Rafe unconsciously fidgeted and shifted his feet in the sand.

They laughed again, swinging their gaze to Lynna who carried the Horn.

"I see the Huntress of the Sea received her prize as well." Finally, they turned their eyes to Bevire. "And welcome, Goddess of Shadows. We are glad you have joined us. We have much work for you." The three women smiled. "Come." And they turned and walked towards the trees where, once again, the forest bent to their will and created a path for them.

Rafe sighed and followed, signalling to his siblings to do the same. Once more, the Grey Sisters led the way to their tree encircled clearing. All six walked into the glade where silver mist swirled around a crystal orb atop an ornate metal stand.

For a moment, Rafe studied the strange object: a three-legged stand—made of filigree metalwork and patterned leaves—with a brazier at the bottom. Its top curved into a half sphere but flattened out to hold a smaller stand and the orb. The crystal itself seemed to glow varying its colour between silver and blue.

He looked up to see the Grey Sisters staring back. "For the Summoning. It is the Oculus Teardrop."

Bevire sucked in breath and exclaimed, "Oh my! Really?"

"Yes, Shadow Goddess, and soon you will be a part of it. We only await one other."

"Someone else is coming?" Rafe asked the question still pondering what an Oculus Teardrop was and why it impressed Bevire.

The Grey Sisters nodded. "The Goddess of the Moon comes. But she moves on her own time."

Suddenly, as if to belay those words, a shimmer of silver streaked out of the sky and the Goddess of the Moon landed in the clearing, skipping across the ground. She stopped by the Grey Sisters and tilted her head at her family.

"You are all here. And not dead."

Rafe moved forward a step. "You sound surprised."

"That you are here, no. Knew she would come," Manume nodded at Lynna, "if she survived the horn."

Then she turned her head to Bevire. "But you, unexpected. Thought you would hide. Hide, hide in your darkness. Away from what you did."

Bevire straightened her posture and snapped, "Well I didn't! And you're one to talk! Considering the things you've done!"

Manume smiled. "True, true. We've both been naughty. Listened to a nasty little bird whisper nasty little things. Someday we should talk about that bird, you and I."

Bevire inhaled sharply and let the breath out slowly. "Perhaps we should. Someday." The two sisters smiled warily at each other.

"You will have to reach someday first, Goddesses." The Grey Sisters intruded on their moment. "But today, we have much work to do. Starting with you, Shadow Goddess."

"Me?" Bevire took a step back, shock in her voice.

"The God of Souls has his Bow. The Sea Huntress, her Horn. We need the Moon Goddess for the Summoning and to hold the spell. You will give the edge to the mortal warriors. Touch their weapons with your shadows. Fight the darkness with darkness."

Bevire smiled. "Like the arrow."

"Yes, but we will give you some help." They shuffled forward and beckoned Bevire to follow. She advanced and they all surrounded the orb. "We will draw a bit of the realms for you to borrow." They smiled, and Bevire matched their grin.

"I see." She turned to Rafe. "What weapons do your ships have?"

"The sailors on all the ships have swords. Some carry knives, and there's the cannon. The *Jewel* also has harpoons."

"Metal things. Good. Easy to infuse with magic." She addressed the Grey Sisters. "Let's begin."

Each of the sister witches put a hand on the Oculus Teardrop. They began to chant, *"Rhwchyn ni i ni iymlad dytywyll. Rhwchyn ni i ni ber i ni drechur Und Chryn Llyd.*"

Three times they intoned the words until the Teardrop began to glow. Slowly, they moved their hands upward. With the ascent of their fingers, energy was drawn from the orb until a trio of smaller power orbs floated above the Oculus Teardrop. The Grey Sisters stared at Bevire, twisted their wrists, and cried, "*Ryd yn ni rhyrwr phwn! Dwies ysy Cysgodin!*"

The energy spheres abruptly flew, slamming into Bevire's body. She convulsed, her limbs jerking, but did not scream or cry out. Rafe took a step forward, but Lynna's hand on his arm restrained him from interfering.

Bevire shook, her body briefly shining in a greyish silver glow, and then she ceased moving, her body settling quietly.

"It is done. Do you feel it? It won't last forever, but long enough."

Bevire nodded. "Yes. This will succeed most wonderfully." She laughed, a sound soft and disturbing. "I'll return then, and get to work." She spun around conjuring her magic, black shadows racing from the forest to surround her. With a cry of, "I'll see you back on the ship!" she disappeared in a swirl of darkness.

Rafe sighed. "Do I want to know what she's doing?"

"I think you know already, and she's giving your mortals a chance to survive the battle." The Grey Sisters cackled, and Manume giggled an echo of their laughter. "Now you two, Captain and Hunter, stand there and there." The three witches pointed at opposite spots two feet from the Oculus Teardrop. Rafe and Lynna moved into place.

The Grey Sisters shuffled outward moving to stand in a semi-circle next to their orb. Manume moved without being asked to position herself opposite the Sisters, creating a loose circle around the sphere and the stand.

"This must be done in stages. First, we must peel back

the tiers between realms to see the beast." The Grey Sisters nodded at Manume, and the four of them placed their hands on the Oculus Teardrop.

Beneath the stand, the brazier burst into life, a flame blazing and smoke twirling upward. The smoke rose and writhed around the Oculus Teardrop, circling a course around the sphere, never climbing higher in the air.

Together all the women chanted, *"Agoryff ordd, Agoryff tyordd. Daynswch yra nifail, yr Und Chryn Llyd."*

The brazier smoke flowed into the Teardrop, twisting inside like a snake to emerge through the top and expand. It spun as it grew and shredded a rift into the air. Through the breach between spaces, a viewing portal developed, and, slowly, Ashetus' prison realm came into focus.

Visible in the shifting smoke was Ashetus, the Terrible One.

The immense ancient being lay on a bed made from thousands of bones, surrounded by hundreds more skeletons and corpses: men, women, monsters and other beings. Each dead body wailed, swaying, shuffling from foot to foot, but never moving from their place, forever bound to Ashetus.

Rafe sharply inhaled and Lynna snarled under her breath. Manume spat on the ground, but the Grey Sisters did nothing. As they watched this creature, its tentacles wriggling, distended body squirming, it rolled. Six red eyes gleamed, and an appendage lashed out wrapping around one of its corpse slaves. The moving body looked a little decayed, slightly bloated, skin peeling, one eye missing, but still retaining most of its flesh along with the tattered remains of a uniform. Ashetus raised the wailing body high above what passed for its head and opened its maw wide. Three rows of razor-sharp fangs gnashed, and the tentacle dropped the now screaming body into its mouth. None of the gods or witches looked away as the teeth chewed rotting flesh and skeletal bone to pulp, swallowing all into its gullet.

"Carrion eater." Manume spat again. "Scavenger. Filthy thing."

"Yes." The voice of the Grey Sisters agreed, their tone soft, almost sad. "We need to end this beast that should never have begun. Do you have what you need? A location? Can you fix the conduit to bring him here?"

She nodded. "I do. I see the one in place. A nudge, a push. He will follow where I lead."

"Then begin."

Manume inhaled and closed her eyes. A sparkle of silver lit up her hair and shimmered across her skin, skipping across the surface of the orb. The rift snapped closed, and the smoke rushed down back into the orb, sucking the moon magic with it. Inside the sphere, they danced together, smoke and silver light, swirling in a tide of a newly born storm, pulling at the threads that bound the prison of Ashetus to the world of mortal men.

Lynna, Rafe, the Grey Sisters, and the Goddess of the Moon all stared at the maelstrom contained within the orb, their gazes never wavering. They stood, caught in the eye of the storm, for hours, minutes, an eternity, the passage of time rushing by and standing still.

Manume's voice broke the spell. "It is done. The conduit is moved. The beast stirs. The beast moves!" She shrieked, laughing and screaming at the same time. "To the west! Fly to the west, brother! Sister to the sea!"

As if a strange tether was snapped, both Rafe and Lynna sprang into action, shooting into the sky in a blaze of magic, headed to where their sister directed. Below them, their ships sailed into a westerly defensive position, Bevire, Goddess of Shadows and Night, standing on the prow of the *Jewel.*

The God of Souls took his stance in the sky while the Goddess of the Sea dove into her element. And they waited.

To the west of Raven Rock, the clouds in the sky

darkened into a drab, repressed colour of charcoal, tinged with a hint of red. The sea began to bubble and churn, black foam spewing into the air. In the ocean, beyond the churning water, Lynna, Bevire, and the ships waited. Rafe stood ready in the sky with a regular arrow notched in his bow. He spun the wooden shaft with his magic for extra potency. The black arrow still hummed in the quiver, held in reserve, awaiting the perfect moment for the kill.

On the island, Manume held the portal conduit in the silver magic of the moon, a grin plastered on her face. Across from her, the Grey Sisters cackled. "He's coming!"

Chapter Twenty-Four

The Rise of Ashetus

Green tentacles coated in pale ooze and red slime broke the ocean's surface. Three, four, six, and then ten tentacles waving and thrashing, trying to snatch at something, anything. The crown of a head surfaced next like a grotesque child being born into the world. Sickly green and bulbous, snaked with black veins, the head pushed out of the water and glared at the world with six crimson eyes, round holes of fire sunk into what passed for its face. At last, its mouth came into view, a pulsing slit salivating and scraping its rows of jagged teeth together.

For a moment, it bobbed like a swollen carcass spit out from the depths of the sea, and then it rolled on its back, swinging the full length of its gigantic body to the surface. It raised a scaled, tapered fish tail and smashed it down against the water. A tidal wave rose and rolled, looming straight up over the sea, and Ashetus roared one word.

"Death!"

The great tail-generated wave swelled higher and higher into a towering wall of water and with it came the dead. Thousands and thousands of bones ascended from the sea, skeletons ancient and brittle, bleached white, some gnawed and broken, some still with bits of hanging flesh. Freshly decayed corpses rose as well. Newly dead flesh in naval uniform or sailor garb and slightly older bodies half-rotted were plucked from their watery graves. Each poor soul wailed, their remains given tainted life and pain.

Ashetus roared again. *"You are mine! This world is mine!"*

"No, Abomination! It is not!" From far above, Rafe shouted his bold challenge and loosed his first magic-tinged arrow. The projectile sped down, down and pierced Ashetus above one of its crimson eyes. The Terrible One screamed, and the whole of Raven Rock shook. The ocean shuddered from surface to bedrock, and the wave of bones shattered. Rafe watched the dead tumble back into the sea and the great beast thrashed in pain. From the corner of his eye, he saw Lynna calm the seas as the ships fought to stay off the rocks.

"It burns! It burns of stars!" Ashetus swung a tentacle and plucked the arrow from its flesh, crushing the small shaft to powder. *"Jailor! Tormentor! Vile God of the Hunt! You will die! You and your Shadow Bird!"* The six eyes of Ashetus stared at Rafe, glaring with an intensity of hatred to destroy worlds, and its tentacles crashed against the sea.

Rafe loosed another arrow and then another to draw the beast's full attention. To bring him closer for the killing shot. One barb pierced a tentacle, and the other plucked out an eye. Ashetus screamed and lashed out sending a wave of water straight up into the air. Rafe dodged the airborne spray, shocked at its aim and power. As he moved in for another shot, he saw Ashetus sink under the water.

Rafe shouted a warning. "Lynna, watch out! He's submerged!"

But it wasn't his sister that the danger stalked.

Suddenly, the sea erupted and Ashetus leapt from the depths into the sky. Its tentacles spread like bony wings, and its tail flapped like a rudder. Around it shimmered a ruddy glow.

Magic.

It hovered in the sky, blotting out sun and clouds only yards away from Rafe. Blood ran from its wounded eye, and its mouth hung open, drool dripping teeth showing. From deep within its belly, something rumbled. A dark, harsh laugh.

Rafe shivered.

"You are not the God of the Hunt for all you hold his Bow." A tentacle wriggled forward, and Rafe slid away having no desire to be touched by the creature.

"You know fear. Good." Ashetus squirmed, and a sound like the long inhale of a breath came from its mouth. *"You smell of him. Of Stars and strange Gods. But not him."*

"No, I am not him." Rafe finally found his voice. He reached behind his shoulder towards the quiver. Ashetus twitched, and Rafe halted his movement. Waiting.

"Little pinpricks. Shot. Survived. Eye will grow back." The creature waved a tentacle and moved closer. *"Didn't kill. Like him."*

Rafe moved his hand closer to the quiver. Ashetus didn't react. Rafe slowly drew the black arrow and notched the bow. Ashetus did nothing. Rafe steadied his breath. "I am not afraid to kill you."

Then its tentacles whipped in front of its body like a shield, blocking a clear aim, a killing shot. Rafe circled around past clouds, trailing blue energy, trying to find an opening. Ashetus kept pace and denied him a chance. He moved closer, and, suddenly, the beast inhaled again.

"Another scent. Familiar scent." A scream resounded, vibrating the air and knocking Rafe off balance. The beast swept forward still screaming, *"You smell of Death!"* It lashed a tentacle at Rafe with tremendous force.

Rafe threw up a shield of magic as Ashetus' blow

landed, smashing him across the sky. His energy protected him from broken bones and a fractured skull, but not from pain and bruises or the edge of Ashetus' limb from striking a glancing blow on his head. He fumbled the bow and arrow, barely managing to keep them from falling into the sea. Over his trajectory he had no control and only succeeded in cushioning his fall with his magic. Into the trees of Raven Rock, he plunged, his descent cutting a new path through the foliage on the far side of the island until he tumbled to a stop on the rocky beach.

As the world spun and the light dimmed, in the distance he heard the wail of a horn.

Chapter Twenty-Five

The Last of the Dead

Lynna watched in shock as Ashetus delivered a vast blow to her brother. She stared at the great beast floating in the sky, fear slithering across her thoughts. Then, beneath her, the sea rumbled and screamed. Fountains of water shot from the depths: waterspouts, waves, geysers, and gushes of spray sending thousands of the dead rising to attack. Swarms swept over the ships and shadow-infused cannon fire boomed from the three ships, echoing sounds of battle. Waves of bones rushed at Lynna, and she—dealing with the loss of Rafe and facing the great beast and his army—frantically blew the Horn.

A howl of mourning blustered out from the instrument, a long note holding sorrow and the surviving echo of forgotten starlight. Its harmony of melancholy raced across the sea building, swelling, cresting to a zenith. It collided with the advancing legions of Ashetus and broke over their numbers penetrating into each bit of rotted flesh, each fragment of bone. It vibrated within them, promising oblivion, the smashing end of their perverted existence.

For a moment, the dead sighed ready to welcome their

undoing. Their numbers halted, and they ceased their assault, suspended in a fragment of time on the edge of realms. Some crumbled to dust or were smashed by swords and cannon. Other bodies sank back under the waves. The Horn shook the enemy to the verge of defeat.

Then Ashetus roared.

And that roar echoed in the throats of a thousand dead, filling bone and corpse with unhallowed supremacy, counteracting the power of the Horn. A howl of the damned reverberated in the bay and across Raven Rock. The Goddess of the Moon screamed in answer, and the Grey Sisters cried out. The crew of the ships cowered before the enemy despite any bravery or determination in their thoughts, and Lynna felt the intense backlash in her blood, in the connection she had with the Horn.

Then the waves of the dead swept over the Goddess of the Sea.

Wailing throngs of skeletons grabbed at her, bony fingers digging into her flesh, pulling her deep into the ocean in a vain attempt to drown her. They grasped for the Horn as she kicked and thrashed, and she clasped it tight to her chest protecting it with her arms. In her ears, she heard the guttural, hissing voices of the dead.

"The Horn. The Horn. Destroy the Horn. Ashetus commands we destroy the Horn."

As they dragged her to the bottom of the sea, her attackers smashed at her with fists, bit her arms with their broken teeth, yanking, tugging, desperate to pry the Horn from her grasp. She kicked at them, battered them with currents and underwater swells, snapped their bones with her teeth, and lashed out with her magic. Yet, for every skeleton she dislodged, another took its place until, in desperation, she twisted, breaking free enough to raise the Horn to her lips.

In pain and tears, she blew a long, loud broken note. A squealing wobble of discord, of sorrow scraping through an infinity of strife and fear smashing down the ages that blasted into the sea. The dead burst off her, tumbling through the water, and she gasped in relief. She swam, trying to escape, but they came at her again with their reaching bones and their wails.

She turned on them with a snarl and blew the Horn once more. From its bell, sounded a challenge. A noise that cut into her as well as her enemy. Lynna's whole body shuddered, her back arched in a spasm of unbounded energy as her power poured out of the Horn, bound into the thunderous tenor of its bellow.

The sea shook with the released magic moving as a spreading wave of power, and, in a blink of an eye, the dead were gone. Nothing more than dust and fragments sinking to the bottom of the ocean. Lynna floated, dazed, unsure of what happened, shocked that the fight ended so abruptly. She closed her eyes letting the soothing water rock her, so tempted to stay, but the prickling of the Horn still called to her.

The battle is not won.

She opened her eyes. Sore and bleeding she swam up to the air, up to the light, to a war that needed to be fought. She surfaced to chaos and thunder.

Another army of the dead were dancing over water and wave as the cannon from the three ships boomed against encroaching swells. Hordes of the dead clung to the vessels sides and rigging while more fought with the crews. Lynna saw wisps of shadow magic arc in the air as sailors' swords sliced through bone and corpse in battles that raged across sea washed decks.

She swept controlled waves against the ships to scrape away the dead clinging to the sides and smashed their bony carcasses into the advancing legions. She then raised the Horn and blew two notes, short and sharp, that shattered against the first tide of attackers still in the sea.

The crack of their bones rebounded across the bay as

the dead fell to the sound of the Horn, their fragmented bodies sinking back to underwater graves. Three waves of Ashetus' soldiers collapsed, but more surged to replace them. As Lynna raised the Horn to battle again, the frantic clanging of a bell broke through the noise and confusion.

Lynna turned instinctively to the *Jewel*, but it was not her bell that clanged. No, it was the *Sprightly Lark* that sounded the alarm. Screams and shouts echoed off the ship as a wave of the dead smashed into the ship and spun it around. Lynna heard panicked voices and cries of 'Help!' and 'Save us!' as three more breakers barrelled towards the ship carrying hundreds of screaming skeletons.

She arched her hand through the sea, trailing verdant magic and a great wave expanded into existence racing to block the attack. Lynna raised the Horn, but suddenly Ashetus roared. His voice sped the air into a force of tremendous wind, knocking Lynna off balance and under the water. She surfaced almost immediately, but not in time.

Above her, Ashetus laughed.

Lynna watched helplessly as two of the waves slammed into the ship, and hordes of the dead overran the *Sprightly Lark*. Her counter wave crashed into the third attack deflecting it and sending the bones back into the sea. She raced to intercept as the sea rolled and rose again.

Lynna called to the ocean, singing out to the water with an undulating cry and brought her element from the depths. A wall of water ascended into the air to form a majestic height of sea and Lynna placed it between the ship and the advancing throng of creatures. She held the line as the attack smashed into her defensive wall, and then pushed forward, slamming again and again against the army of the dead, crushing all that came against her and sending their remains into the deeps.

Still, it was not enough to save the *Sprightly Lark*.

Behind her, she heard the loud, ear-splitting crack of

rending wood. She spun to see the *Sprightly Lark* pointed bow first towards the shore, smashed against the rocks with her port side gashed open, and the ship taking on water. Skeletons and corpses swarmed the ship, attacking sailors, pulling men into the water to drown. On the listing quarterdeck, she saw Commander Vaughan swinging his sword through a mass of snarling bones.

With a cry and a breath, Lynna commanded the ocean. She brought waves crashing over the ship, plucking the sailors from the clutches of the dead into the surf. Eddies swirled inside the broken vessel at her command and pulled out men trapped in its bowels. At her direction, the sea plucked all still living from the clutches of death and set them careening to the shore to wash up on the sand.

Then she turned on the dead.

She heaved the attackers of the *Sprightly Lark* high into the air in gushing sprays of sea, smashing them into oblivion against the circling form of Ashetus. The beast howled in pain, peppered and speared in bits of broken bone. Blood dripped and smeared across his skin, another eye pierced by a fractured arm bone. He flourished his tentacles and yanked the fragments of the dead from his bloated body tossing the bloodied bits into his mouth and crunching them between his teeth.

Below the beast, Lynna closed her eyes. She submerged just below the surface and blew all her fury into the Horn.

A cacophonous squall broke, booming across the ocean up and out of the water into the sky. It struck all the congregated dead in the sea and on the ships like a battering ram, smashing into them as a solid geyser of sound. It ripped them apart, pulverizing decay and bone, turning the shouts of the living into the screams of the dead.

In the span of a lap of the tide on the shore, the army of the dead collapsed, transforming into powder floating on the sea. From the sky, their master watched.

As the last of its slaves, its dead, turned to dust, the Terrible One yowled and descended from the sky. Ashetus spun, a whirligig of fury, splattering blood, and mocking laughter, its tentacles lashing out creating a rotating circle. It dove towards the sea, a limb nearly crushing the top of the *Jewel's* main mast, and another carving a gouge in the foremast of the *Star's Hope*. The great beast skimmed the surface of the bay racing straight for Lynna.

She rose on a massive sea wave to meet it, her face alive in defiance, her body draped in an emerald glow of magic, and the Horn at her lips. She blew a trumpet blast, a perfect note of the wild, powerful sea, and sounded her challenge to the Terrible One.

The howl of a hurricane melded with the crash of the pounding surf as the thundering music of the Horn filled the air. It washed over god, beast, and sailor in a lifting tide, cutting deep into the essence of each living being present. Cries of awe and bravado rose from the ships and beach, and, from the Terrible One, came an answering roar of pain and fury.

"It burns! Burns! Vile Horn!" Ashetus swiftly changed course, breaking off his attacking run on Lynna and climbed into the sky. He thrashed his limbs and ground his teeth, and gusts of wind swept across the sea.

Lynna spun a giant waterspout and ascended far above the water. In swirling sea and foam, she stood far above Raven Rock, rage and fear warring in her face as she stared at Ashetus. She shuddered at the sight of it, wriggling tentacles and rows of teeth under cruel red eyes. Every scrap of dread, anger, and horror she felt burst out in a scream.

"Abomination!"

Ashetus stilled, its body stopped moving. It looked at Lynna with its eyes, a hint of confusion within his gaze. Its voice growled up from its belly.

"Death called me that. Once." It clicked its teeth, drool

spilling out. "She said, 'Abomination' and cast me out." A laugh rumbled. "But I showed her. I am Abomination. And more. I am more than Death." Ashetus shook, his body quaking in cruel and dreadful laughter.

Lynna snarled under her breath and felt the Horn quiver in her hand, calling for her to use it, calling for her to end the thing before her. She brought it to her lips and sounded its song.

At the touch of the first note, the space between sky and sea keened in boundless beauty, in a story of never-ending starlight and tranquillity, of the first meeting of eternity and death. The Horn blew a melody of sorrow wrapped in a sigh, snatched from the first hope of life and encircled past the world's finality. The sound of the Horn shook the fabric of the realms and pierced the soul of every creature. It cut to the heart of darkness and shone warm starlight into the abyss.

Ashetus screamed.

And with him, the world.

The echo of his voice chased the reverberation of the Horn, striking dread and terror into the farthest corners of the Outer Islands. Every man and god at Raven Rock and beyond trembled. Every soul in the After World cringed in fear.

Lynna gasped in the shock of it all, and her control wavered. Her magic faltered. The waterspout collapsed and she fell, only just breaking her descent with a hastily conjured wave. She was swept back under the sea before surfacing to find the rapidly plunging form of Ashetus falling toward her.

She blew the Horn, another powerful blast straight at Ashetus.

It shrieked and veered away but lashed out with its tentacles. Green slimy tips smashed into her arm and shoulder and the Horn went flying from her grasp. It rose into the air in an arch, tumbling like a seashell tossed from the beach as Lynna cried out in panic.

She spun upward on a geyser of water in a desperate attempt to retrieve it as Ashetus spied the Horn. It growled, *"Destroy!"* and swung a tentacle through the air. Lynna's fingers grasped for the Horn, only inches from her goal, but too late. The beast struck the instrument with all its power and smashed the Horn of the Gods into pieces.

Lynna shrieked, "No!" as a rain of white shards fell into the sea. She dodged another blow from Ashetus and dove back to her domain, chasing the broken Horn into the ocean.

Sprawled in the underbrush, bruised and bleeding, Rafe's mind drifted in the dark unconscious as the battle raged just beyond Raven Rock. His body pressed against the earth, his heartbeat thumping a steady beat and his breath even. Yet he lay still, lost in oblivion.

A breeze rustled the trees, sweeping down to brush against his hair. In the distance, the sea washed along the beach, and, from the sky, a sliver of moonlight descended to whisper in his ear.

"Wake up."

Rafe stirred, but his eyes remained closed.

The moonlight danced along his skin scattering stardust over his eyes. It whispered again.

"Wake up."

Rafe's fingers twitched, and he moaned. His eyelids fluttered. Twinkles of stardust shimmered over his face. Somewhere on the edge of oblivion, his blood stirred, and his mind crawled from the darkness.

"Wake up. Foolish brother."

His eyelids fluttered again, and his eyes blinked open. The sliver of moonlight vanished, and Rafe stared at the sky shadowed by the trees. In the distance, he heard shrieks and the final echo of a horn.

He groaned and pushed himself into a sitting position, his body aching and his head throbbing. His first coherent thoughts were of the Bow and the black arrow. He strained to focus his eyes, hands scrabbling as he searched the ground, a sigh of relief coming when he found the weapons unharmed nearby. He snatched them up and rose unsteadily to his feet. He leaned against a tree to get his bearings, his headache eased if still thumping a beat inside his skull. He touched his forehead. Bits of dried blood rubbed off onto his fingers.

He took a breath, then another, slowly brushing away the fog and reconnected with the magic in his blood. A blue glow lit his skin, growing stronger with each breath, and he rose in the air. He hovered for a few moments and then ascended above the treetops, to rejoin the battle.

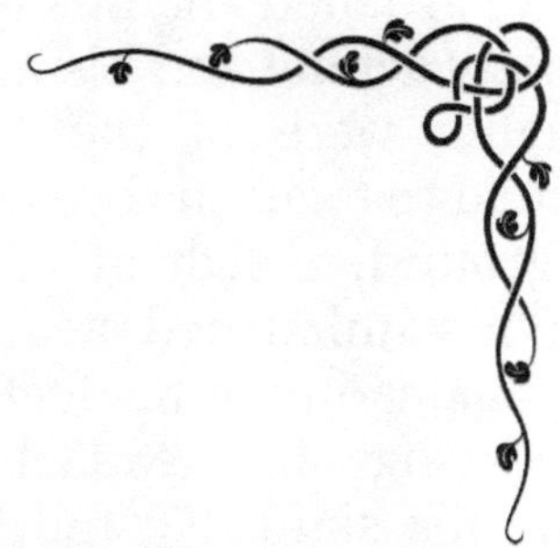

Chapter Twenty-Six

Old Enemies

Lynna, Bevire, and the crew of the remaining ships watched in horror as the pieces of the horn sunk beneath the water with the remains of the dead it destroyed. Above them, the Terrible One hovered, grinning, drool falling like drops of rain.

Its voice rumbled, *"Now you die!"*

Instinctively, like a little whisper in her ear, Bevire cast a veil of shadows between them and Ashetus in a desperate attempt to hide everyone from sight. A barrier of darkness shrouded the sea and sky turning daylight into night and Raven Rock into a hidden sanctuary.

Ashetus batted at the shadow cover with its limbs growling, confused at the sudden gloom. It squirmed around moving to the left, then right, twisting and moving backward, out to sea.

"Tricks!" It shrieked. *"Tricks won't save you!"*

A murmur of breath brushed against the creature's thoughts. "No. But they're not the ones needing to be saved."

From the charcoal clouds, swooped a bird, a crow, along

the edge of shadows straight towards Ashetus, his black on black invisible to all. As it flew, the crow snatched a small filament of Bevire's magic in its beak, twisting the shadow with its own red power in a strand woven to a particular task. The Crow soared in a wide circle around the Terrible One, looping the magic in its wake and then, repeating its flight, winding ring after ring. The Nightmare Crow wove a net, a prison, and bound the beast in the shadow of time cutting it off from the outside world. Blinded by the loss of two eyes and the darkness, the beast never realized its doom until the crow snapped the constraint in place and it tightened inward around Ashetus, confining the creature. Then the crow laughed.

"Now we are alone, Ashetus. Only you and I. Suspended in time between realms."

"Shadow Bird!" The beast roared and swung a tentacle at the voice cackling from the darkness. The appendage moved but an inch, restrained by the Crow's spell working. Ashetus roared again, writhing, doing little more than shaking in place, dangling inside the rings like a toy.

"Still full of rage and bluster and still a beast. I'll enjoy watching you die." The Crow flew close enough for Ashetus to see him.

"No. I will see you die. I will enjoy crushing you in my jaws." The Terrible One gnashed its teeth. *"You cannot kill me. You have not the power."*

"You are right." The Nightmare Crow fluttered his wings, wisps of shadow dancing around his head. "I cannot kill you." The bird gently chuckled. "But that is not why I brought you here."

A flap of wing and the bird wheeled, soaring up and over Ashetus and then diving down straight at his foe. From the bird's feet extended strange silver talons, and he sunk those claws deep into the creature's head. The puncture wounds oozed black blood and greenish pus. Both Ashetus and the Crow screamed: one in pain, the other in triumph.

The Crow shouted the words, *"Rwynd wynwer! Rwyncym rydyr hyndd yledus!"*

A great growl ripped out of the throat of Ashetus. *"What are you doing, Shadow Bird?"*

"Taking my due! My revenge!"

Scarlet and burnt orange streaks snaked across Ashetus' flesh, throbbing and pulsing in energy. Its body jerked in convulsions as raw power poured from the wounds that the Crow made, the grand dark magic of Ashetus sucked from the beast and absorbed by the Nightmare Crow.

Ashetus howled, *"Noooo! It burns! It burns! Stop it!"* It thrashed, trying to dislodge the bird, but the shadow rings held it tight.

"Stop it! Stop! Stop!" A breath, a yowl, and then, *"Please stop! Not again! Bad Shadow Bird!"*

The Crow only dug its claws deeper, yanking the power from Ashetus faster.

"Nooo!" A wail ripped the air, and Ashetus shook like a child tormented. *"Please stop! Please! Shadow Bird hurts! It hurts! Father hurts me! Please stop! Father, please!"*

For a moment, the Crow wavered, an old emotion stirring. Then he snapped his beak and shrieked, "No! No longer! I am never that again!" A caw escaped his throat, long, harsh and full of pain."I will never be that again! You snapped that tie, oh horrid beast, when you broke your mother's heart! When you killed your uncles! When you turned Ulerne's heart against me!"

The Crow dug his claws in deeper, and, with a roar, continued siphoning the magic from the creature he once called his son. He wrenched the energy from its flesh, drained its power, absorbing every drop into his body, making the Crow replete and strong with the stolen magic. Soon, Ashetus ceased struggling, ceased howling, soon it became weak and listless. Alive, but with only a hint of the power it once possessed.

Sated, glowing in power, the Crow whispered, "Now

he comes for you. The one that smells of Death. Your brother."

Ashetus groaned, its voice slurred. *"No. Father is wrong. I am the only son of Death. No brother."*

"Oh yes, Terrible One, you have a brother. He comes to kill you. And you will die."

With a laugh, the Nightmare Crow released its talons and flew straight up into the clouds. As he rose, the bird snatched a piece of the shadow rings sweeping away his bindings and brushing away Bevire's darkness. Ashetus was revealed to the world, still hanging in the sky, a groan in its throat, its limp tentacles swaying in the air, and its eyes closing. The Crow left as he came, unseen and on the wind.

The wind brought something else from the island. A battered god, swirling upward on a tide of magic. Surrounded by a blue glow, Rafe washed across the sky, the Bow at the ready, notched with the black shadow arrow. Banged and bruised, blood smeared on his forehead, he called out his enemy.

"Open your eyes Ashetus!"

A moan came from the creature, and, slowly, one by one, its five remaining eyes gaped open. Rafe stared at Ashetus, and confusion seemed to stare back from its clouded orbs. Its tentacles swung back and forth, but it made no attempt to move.

"God of the Hunt. With your small Bow. And your smaller Crow." A growling laugh coughed out of its belly. *"Bah. Spells, pinpricks. It means nothing. Take what you will. I will survive. I am not afraid. You will not kill me. You are weak. I will crush your bones. Crush you all in the end."*

Rafe took a breath, pulling back on the bow's string. "I am not the Hunter." He let the black arrow fly.

Straight and true it soared, and Ashetus watched it come, its fanged mouth wide, a laugh roaring in the wind.

Through an eye it stabbed, the arrow piercing membrane deep into the flesh beneath. A raging scream replaced the laugh as shadow and starlight burned into the Terrible One's veins. The beast went rigid, a silver glow consuming it, and black flames shattered through skin. Putrid, oily smoke stinking of fish and rot filled the air, and chunks of crispy flesh fell into the sea. Black fire and a silver glare lit up the sky like a daylight moon burning inside an obsidian sun.

Then a sound reverberated across the air, a shockwave of blood-chilling torture that spun Rafe away from the blazing form of Ashetus. With a start, Rafe realized the noise was a death cry. The last howl of a would-be destroyer of worlds. As its wail vibrated over the area, Rafe wrapped himself in a blue flare of magic and descended. He watched the final yowl of Ashetus bend the treetops of Raven Rock and stir the sea into roiling waves.

And then everything went silent.

He looked up. Flaming rain fell, sizzling as it hit the water. He saw his sisters conjure shields of shadow and sea to protect the men and ships under their care and flew to help. His magic flashed, extending across the bay and the island, a shelter against the downward conflagration of debris. Together, the three gods held against the demise of Ashetus until the last remains of his carcass sunk beneath the ocean. And somewhere in the Realm of Death, a mother held out her arms. She sang a soft lullaby to the lost son returned to her.

Back in the realm of mortals, as magic faded among the steam drifting off the water, cheers rose up from the beach and the two ships. Only then did Rafe see the wreck of the *Sprightly Lark* half submerged on the rocks east of the bay. He studied the *Jewel*, his heart at ease when he spied her still well and relatively undamaged. He drifted down to the sand as Lynna came to shore. He noticed that she came empty-handed but smiling.

"You did it!" She spun around as she reached the beach, spraying sand and tide in a gleeful display. "He's dead! It's over!"

"He is. The world's safe." Rafe slung the bow he carried over the quiver on his shoulder. "But I fear I missed the worst of the battle." He nodded towards the shipwreck. "I'm sorry."

"We held our own." She glanced at the now jubilant naval sailors on the beach. "We all did." Then she sighed. "But I lost the Horn. Ashetus destroyed it. Shattered it to pieces. The Horn's remains keep the dead company at the bottom of the sea."

"That may be for the best. Something that powerful..." He grimaced. "As it is, I will have to find a place to hide the Bow."

"To the Isle of Shadows, perhaps?"

"Never." The word snapped out with force from behind them as the lilting voice of the Goddess of the Moon broke into the conversation. Then more softly came, "Never. Bad thoughts. Bad, bad, bad. Not for gods anymore, that Bow."

Rafe turned to see Manume and the Grey Sisters walk out of the trees and strolled to meet them. His sister came to his side and tilted her head, silver hair blowing in the wind. "You did a good thing. Remember that. The other thing needed to happen." Then she skipped away, flew into the air on a tide of silver to disappear in a flash of light.

Rafe turned to the Grey Sisters. "Should I ask what that was about?"

"Best not. You'll sleep more soundly." They laughed and then said, "We've come for the Bow." The three women each held out a hand.

For a moment, Rafe thought about refusing before retrieving the weapon and handing it to the women. "You'll most likely do a better job at seeing this disappears again."

"We will. And if you ever have need of it again, you know where to come this time. No more chasing songs and whispers." The women cackled and then left, disappearing into the trees.

"Do you need me anymore?" Lynna's voice pulled his attention back from his thoughts. "If not, I want to return home, spread the word to my sea creatures that it's safe to come back, that the threat is gone."

"Are the other ships seaworthy?" Lynna nodded. "Then go, I'll get the men here on the beach to the vessels and back to the islands. And thank you."

"You're welcome." Lynna smiled, a glint of impishness in her eye. "Just don't expect me to come bail you out of trouble every time, brother." She laughed and raced back into the sea. As she swam away, she shouted, "Do tell that nice Pelham fellow good-bye. I *will* see him again." With another laugh, she dove under the waves and from Rafe's sight.

Rafe sighed and hoped his sister was teasing him. A part of him shuddered at the thought of a possible friendship between Lynna and Pelham.

"Captain, look!" He turned his head at the sound of Commander Vaughan's voice and pulled his gaze towards the waiting ships. Several long boats were lowering off the vessels.

"Well, lads, it looks like rescue is coming to us. We'll soon get you on home."

Chapter Twenty-Seven

Set Sails

Blackthorne was first out of the longboats when they landed at the beach and headed straight for Rafe. "Glad to see you're in one piece, sir. I feared the worst after you were struck by the beast."

"So did I for few moments. Luckily, I managed to shield myself from the brunt of it." He flashed a rueful grin. "I missed most of the battle, though. What happened? Injuries? Casualties?"

Blackthorne glanced over at the navy men now milling around the longboats. "The *Sprightly Lark* took the worst blow, as you can see. She got hit by two companies of those dead men, and waves washed her port side into the rocks. Lynna got the men you see here to shore, but we lost some. The bodies got pulled under by the dead, and I didn't see a trace of their souls." Blackthorne sighed.

"I wouldn't worry on that account," Rafe reassured. "The After World is righting itself. I can feel it. Souls will find their way home, I think."

"Good to hear that, at least. We've enough to deal with." He nodded at the shipwreck. "It looks bad, but the navy ship might be salvageable. It's wedged well on the rocky coast, and I doubt the tide will pull her further under. The gash in her side can be fixed, I think, if the bottom and the keel are intact."

"What of the *Jewel* and *Star's Hope?* And Bevire?"

"The *Jewel* took some damage, but nothing we haven't weathered before. And we didn't lose a man." Blackthorne paused, looking distinctly uncomfortable. Then he almost spat the words. "As much as it pains me to say it, Pelham and his ship were a stellar crew and fought bravely. They lost a few men, but not many. It makes it harder to dislike the man, fighting alongside him."

"Yes, I think we may have to call a truce in regard to Commander Pelham."

Blackthorne scowled. "We'll see. As to your sister, sir, she and her magic gave us the edge, it did. Don't know what blasted conjuring she did to our weapons, but they cut through the skeletons and the corpses like a ship through calm seas. It's a shame we can't keep the spell, but she was a bit adamant about that. She's tending to that task at the moment. Relieving the ships' weapons of her added magic." He sighed. "You might have noticed none of us are carrying blades, sir. That's why. She will want to see the returning men about that as well."

Rafe grinned. "It may seem a shame, but trust me, you don't want to carry around my sister's magic. It can be... unpredictable...over time."

Blackthorne shrugged. Rafe clapped him on the shoulder. "Let's get these men back on to our ships and set sail to the nearest navy port then we can properly celebrate with some rum."

"Aye, sir." Blackthorne grinned, and the pair walked to the longboats. They oversaw an orderly loading of the boat, and the first group rowed away from the beach. A few more trips, and, at last, their turn came to row back to the *Jewel*. Rafe watched his ship grow closer with a feeling of relief and joy and grinned in delight when he finally felt the deck boards beneath his boots.

He walked up to the quarterdeck to a chorus of cheers and surveyed his ship. One-Eyed Anders grinned at him from the helm, winking his one good eye. Rafe watched the crew: some of his men settling the naval newcomers into the routine, others repairing damaged rigging, sail and deck. His sister stood by the prow, siphoning off the last of the borrowed magic from blades. His blood itched to set sail, but he knew he must be patient. Neither the ships nor the crews were yet ready.

He turned his head to look out at the *Star's Hope* seeing Pelham standing on his quarterdeck, a momentary reflection of himself. The sun danced off the clouds against the bluest sky. One would never know the death that rose and fell against this backdrop.

Rafe sighed and murmured. "I wonder how they'll write about it in the books? Or will they even remember?"

"Someone will. We gods are long-lived, brother." Rafe turned around to see Bevire standing behind him, somehow sneaking across the deck without a sound. She smiled. "I just wanted to say goodbye. I have retrieved the last of the magic from your ship and crew. I have a few more to chase down over there," she nodded at the *Star's Hope.* "And then I'm leaving. Back to my sanctuary."

Rafe nodded. "Thank you. I know this was difficult for you."

"Not as much as I supposed. And any difficulties, I deserved." She dropped her voice to a whisper. "I never meant any of this to happen. Know that."

"I know. We are good, you and I."

She smiled. "We are." Shadows swirled from all the deep corners of the ship, converging on Bevire. She floated up and over the rail, ready to journey across the water to the *Star's Hope.* She paused for a moment as she cleared the railing. "Though you still owe me a night's sail, brother.

Someday." She smiled and sped away, trailing wind and wisps of shadow.

"Quite the adventure, sir." Blackthorne appeared at his elbow carrying two small glasses of amber liquid. "I believe you said something about rum, sir." He handed a glass to Rafe who grinned.

"I believe I did." The captain took the glass and sipped. The liquor burned a welcome path down his throat. "So, what's the damage? How long before we can sail?"

"Minor, sir, and, with the extra crew, we'll be good inside of an hour or two. It'll be longer, though, if you want to wait for Pelham. His ship took more damage."

Rafe glanced at the position of the sun in the sky. "That may put the hour rather late." Reluctantly he added, "Maybe we should consider staying in port at Raven Rock until tomorrow."

"Begging your pardon, sir, neither crew wants to stay in port here for the night. However late the hour, as soon as we're able, both ships want to sail. Even if we face night sailing. And Storm Point or the Stone Fire Islands aren't that far."

"Very well." Inwardly Rafe smiled, relieved. He had no desire to linger at Raven Rock either.

"Sir." Blackthorne's voice paused, holding a note of unwillingness to voice his thoughts. Rafe waited patiently until the man continued. "Is this the end of our troubles? It seems not to me."

Surprised, Rafe asked, "Why? Ashetus is dead. The worlds are safe."

"Are they? The creature truly behind this, the Nightmare Crow, is still out there. And..." Blackthorne turned his head towards the sea.

"What is it?"

"Something happened during the battle. After the horn was destroyed. Bevire cast her shadows to hide us, but—It shouldn't have stopped it, sir. Ashetus should have attacked. But it didn't. And when the shadows vanished, Bevire seemed surprised. She didn't lift them, and I don't think Ashetus did either. I think some other force was at work. And..." He drowned the rest of his words in a swig of rum.

"And what, Blackthorne."

"I think it was the Crow. I don't think he's done with us yet, sir. I don't."

Rafe sighed. "I wish I didn't agree, old friend, but I fear you are right."

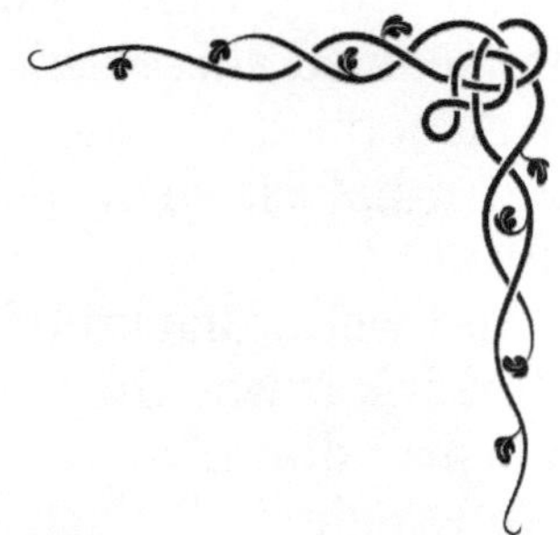

Epilogue

The wind blew a hint of salt air and the fresh smell of night blooming roses. Overhead, the soft light of an ever-shining moon sparkled its radiance among the treetops. A *whoosh* of air tracked a faint echo in the clouds, and the flutter of wings gently settled on a topmost branch of a tree.

The Nightmare Crow looked up at the moon and the pinpricks of stars in the canopy of the sky. He knew the name of each constellation, each luminescent gateway that dotted the black sky. He stared at them, their names itching on his tongue, the burning memory of his other home tumbling through his thoughts. He missed the sweet comfort of the stars.

He spread his wings and let out a breath. He spoke to the night, softly, sadly. "I should be there, beyond this cold, dark world. I should be in the light. I should be among the stars." He fanned his wings, letting the wind ruffle his feathers. Then he cawed, harsh and strident, screaming to the world.

"I flew between heartbeats, between eons in time, along the pathways to see the shine of starlight! And now! Now?" The tree branch shook under the weight of his anger. "Now

I am trapped in this form, cast aside like filth under your feet! Abandoned on this world! Shut away from the stars!"

The Crow closed his eyes and then opened them, calming his rage. He stared once more at the stars. "You did this to me. *Hunter*. Great and mighty. False friend." He cawed, bitter anger in the sound. "You wronged me, Hunter. Wronged us all with your quest." The Crow spat.

"You led us back down to this muck of a world, my brothers and I. We followed willingly. We trusted you." The Crow's eyes glittered in a sheen of tears reflecting moonlight. "All those years ago. You led us to death and then turned your back. Left me as this pitiful shell of what I was, and my brothers gone." His wings swayed, fanning the air. "I know you can hear me up there in the stars. I know you see me. You think me weak, but no longer. I have taken back what was mine. I have avenged my brothers. Soon it will be your turn. My game is coming to its end."

The bird chuckled and settled down to sleep. As he nestled to roost, head bowed, wings tucked by his sides, the wind blew through the leaves of the trees. Shards of radiance shone down from the sky, the reflected light of the moon and stars dancing diamonds over his black feathers.

A Brief History of the Gods

Interpreted from the Writings of Osratis
Property of Lord Merrill

In the Time of the World Before the Light, there was Death.

She ruled the lands and seas, and the world knew its place in Chaos.

In the Time of the World Before the Light, there was Eternal Night.

Darkness covered the land and seas in stillness and a timeless void.

The creatures of the world existed between Death and Darkness, lost in a measure of shifting realms, of life outside the dominion of the beings we call gods. In the Night they drifted under muted Moon, voices calling, the static air singing to all: monsters, giants, serpents, misshapen things of terrifying beauty and more. And in the smallest part of this world lived mortal men.

How long the world of Death and Darkness existed no one knows. An eon, a second, a breath of time in an ocean of eternity. The world simply existed in life and its end and life reborn.

In the Time of the World Before the Light, there was Death.

And Death changed the world.
Death fell in love.

With whom or what is lost to time and memory, though some say he flew on the wings of shadow and nightmare. All that is known is a child came from the union of Death and her paramour. A being like her of shadow and night, of mortality and endings, but yet...a child of flesh and substance, a child of the corporeal world.

She named the child *Ashetus*.

Soon he would have another name.

Ashetus grew, as children will, as the darling of his mother, coddled, doted on, and loved. He followed her path through the world like a pup at his master's heel. He watched her, saw Death in all her glory, studied mortal and monster alike as they fell into her arms with their last breath.

And he grew envious.

Envious of her stolen attention, jealous of her power. He craved what she had. He craved the touch of Death. He wanted to both embrace it and wield it. It festered in his soul, in his heart, this envy, this greedy desire. And slowly it ate at him, transforming him.

Until one day his mother looked upon him. Until the day Death truly looked upon what her son had become. That is the day the world changed.

I do not know you, my son.
You are beast! You are Abomination!

Death raised her hand to strike, but could not end her son.

Ashetus fled in the Eternal Night.

Fled into the faraway seas.

There, in the black waters, in the cold touch of Night, he succumbed to all his envy, all his greed, all his anger.

There, he let loose his power. The perfection of his form shattered, giving way to monster, to eyes of crimson and grasping tentacles. To blood black and cold and skin a sickly green.

And he laughed.

Thus began his reign of the worlds, the reign of Ashetus.

The Terrible One.

In the Time of the World Before the Light, there was the Terrible One.

He stalked the lands and seas, and the world knew horror.

In the Time of the World Before the Light, there was Eternal Pain.

Darkness covered the land and seas in screaming and timeless torture.

The Realm of Eternal Night descended past Chaos, past Death, into Fear. Every monster, giant, serpent, misshapen thing and mortal creature became prey or slave. All were pursued, quarry to be consumed. Flesh to feed the hunger of Ashetus for death. Those unlucky enough to be caught had their broken bodies picked clean of flesh, and their bones fashioned into his bed or into undying slaves. One by one, the creatures of the Darkness fell to Ashetus, their screams forever echoing on the winds of the worlds.

Everywhere voices shrieked, calling for escape, for the end...

In the Time of the World Before the Light, the stars heard the screams.

In the Time of the World Before the Light, the Hunter answered the call.

He came riding on starlight from the sky, in the

company of the three Shadow Birds. Into the Eternal Night, he came lighting the world for the first time. Past the seas turned blue, through the air now sparkling with radiance to land upon the ground fresh in emerald green. His feet hit the earth with a thunderous *crack* and the lands shook with the force of his power. The ground split asunder and flung chunks out into the seas.

This woke Ashetus.

When Light Came to the World, the Hunter battled the Army of Bones
When Light Came to the World, the Hunter battled the Terrible One.
The dead fell to the Horn of the Gods
The Shadow Birds died, save one.
Ashetus fell, wounded by the Bow of the Hunter.

It is said that Death herself appeared then as the Hunter raised his Bow for the killing shot. It is said she begged the Hunter to spare her son's life. It is said the Hunter was moved by her pleas and showed mercy. Perhaps it is true, perhaps it is not. It is also said she begged him to kill her son, and he rejected her plea. Or the Beasts of the Realm begged the Hunter for the death of Ashetus, and he refused. Some even say that the Hunter heard no plea, gave no reason, simply refused to kill the beast.

The only truth we know is the Terrible One was imprisoned and the monsters—giants, serpents, and misshapen things—were banished to a place called the Archipelago of Nightfall, a place where the Eternal Night continued to exist.

The rest of the world was given to the mortals...

When Light Came to the World, the Outer Islands were born
When Light Came to the World, the Seven Kingdoms

were born

When Light Came to the World, Death created the After World

When Light Came to the World, the Hunter gave us gods.

When Light Came to the World, the Hunter brought us his son.

When Light Came to the World...so did destiny.

Pronunciation Guide

A partial list of name pronunciation

Manume –Man-You-May
Lynna –Lin-Ah
Bevire –Bev-ear
Abersythe –Ab-Er-Sigh-th
Llansfoot –Lans-foot
Amaratha –Am-Ara-Tha
Ashetus –Ash-et-us
Ulerne –Ool earn
Reis –Ray-iss
Jainna –Jay-na

Rafe's Family Tree

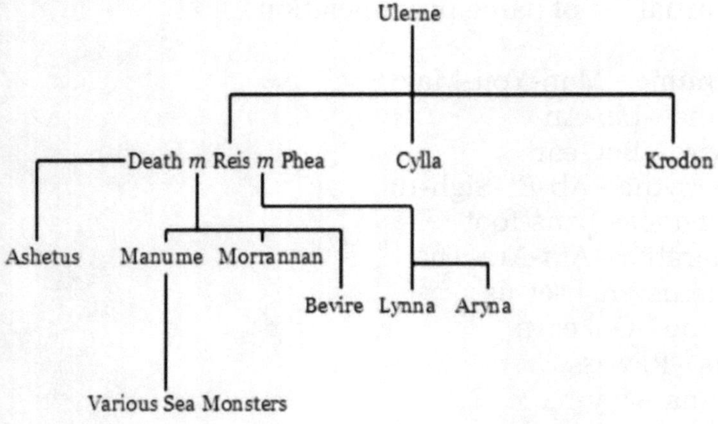

About the Author

A steadfast and proud sci-fi and fantasy geek, A. F. Stewart was born and raised in Nova Scotia, Canada and still calls it home. The youngest in a family of seven children, she always had an overly creative mind and an active imagination. She favours the dark and deadly when writing—her genres of choice being dark fantasy and horror—but she has been known to venture into the light on occasion. As an indie author she's published novellas and story collections, with a few side trips into poetry.